THE WIZARD OF THE KREMLIN

THE
WIZARD
OF THE
KREMLIN

Giuliano da Empoli

TRANSLATED FROM
THE FRENCH BY WILLARD WOOD

Other Press
New York

Originally published in French as *Le mage du Kremlin* in 2022
by Éditions Gallimard, Paris

Copyright © Éditions Gallimard, 2022

Translation copyright © Willard Wood, 2023

Title-page art by StockLeb / Shutterstock.
Quoted passages are from the following sources:
"Letter to Stalin," from *A Soviet Heretic: Essays by Yevgeny Zamyatin*.
Translated by Mirra Ginsburg. Chicago: University of Chicago Press, 1970.
Right and Left, by Joseph Roth. Translated by Michael Hofmann.
New York: Overlook Press, 1992, 2004. Quotation modified
by Willard Wood.
We, by Yevgeny Zamyatin. Translated by Gregory Zilboorg.
New York: Dutton, 1924.

Production editor: Yvonne E. Cárdenas
This book was set in Bembo by
Alpha Design & Composition of Pittsfield,NH

3 5 7 9 10 8 6 4 2

Library of Congress Cataloging-in-Publication Data
Names: Da Empoli, Giuliano, author. | Wood, Willard, translator.
Title: The wizard of the Kremlin : a novel / Giuliano da Empoli ;
translated from the French by Willard Wood.
Other titles: Mage du Kremlin. English
Description: New York : Other Press, [2023]
Identifiers: LCCN 2023008500 (print) | LCCN 2023008501 (ebook) |
ISBN 9781635423952 (paperback ; acid-free paper) |
ISBN 9781635423969 (ebook)
Subjects: LCGFT: Novels.
Classification: LCC PQ2704.A34 M3413 2023 (print) |
LCC PQ2704.A34 (ebook) | DDC 843/.92—dc23/eng/20230224
LC record available at https://lccn.loc.gov/2023008500
LC ebook record available at https://lccn.loc.gov/2023008501

Publisher's Note

Though this novel was inspired by real-life individuals and events, the characters' private lives and dialogue are fictitious, as are the incidents described
throughout.

For Alma

Life is a comedy. One must play it seriously.

—ALEXANDRE KOJÈVE

I

FOR A LONG TIME, the most disparate reports had been circulating about him. Some said he'd retired to a monastery on Mount Athos to pray among the rocks and lizards, others swore they'd seen him partying at a villa in Sotogrande with a cast of coked-up supermodels. Still others said he'd been spotted on a runway at the Sharjah airport, at the militia headquarters in the Donbas, or wandering the ruins of Mogadishu.

Since Vadim Baranov quit his post as advisor to the tsar, stories about him had been multiplying rather than fading away. This happens sometimes. For the most part, men in power derive their aura from the position they hold. When they lose it, it's as if a plug had been pulled. They deflate like one of those giant puppets at the entrance to amusement parks, and if you see these men in the street you wonder how they ever stirred such passions.

Baranov was of a different order. What order that might be, though, I'd be hard-pressed to say. In photographs, he seemed sturdily built but not athletic, always dressed in dark, slightly overlarge suits. His face was ordinary, somewhat boyish, with a pale complexion, and his straight black hair was cut like a schoolboy's. A video taken on the fringes of an official meeting showed him laughing, a rare sight in Russia, where even a smile is considered a sign of idiocy. In fact, he seemed to pay no attention whatever to his appearance—surprising, considering that his stock-in-trade was exactly that, setting mirrors in a circle so that a spark could become a wildfire.

Baranov went through life surrounded by mysteries. The one thing about him that was more or less certain was his influence over the tsar. In his fifteen years of service to him, he'd helped build up the man's power considerably.

He was called the "Wizard of the Kremlin," and the "new Rasputin." At the time, his role was not clearly defined. He would show up in the president's office when the business of the day was done. It wasn't the secretaries who'd called him. Maybe the tsar himself had summoned him on his direct line. Or he'd guessed the right time on his own, thanks to his extraordinary talents, which everyone acknowledged without being able to say exactly what they were. Sometimes a third person would join them, a minister enjoying a moment in the limelight or the boss of a state company.

But given that no one ever says anything in Moscow as a matter of principle, and this goes back centuries, even the presence of these occasional witnesses failed to shed light on the nocturnal activities of the tsar and his advisor. Yet the consequences sometimes stood out clearly. One morning, all Russia awoke to learn that the richest and best-known businessman in the country, the symbol of the new capitalism, had been arrested. Another time, all the presidents of the federal republics, duly elected by the people, had been dismissed, and the morning newscasts informed their still-drowsy audience that from now on the tsar would appoint the presidents himself. In most cases, though, these late-night sessions produced no visible effect. Only years later would changes occur, as though naturally, but in fact as the result of meticulous planning.

At that time, Baranov lived very privately. You never saw him anywhere, and an interview was out of the question. He did have one quirk, though. From time to time he would publish something, either a brief essay in an obscure independent journal, or a research article on military strategy aimed at the highest echelons of the army, or even a piece of fiction that showed off his talent for paradox, in the best Russian tradition. He never wrote under his own name, but he interspersed his texts with allusions that offered clues about the new world that was taking shape in the late-night Kremlin sessions. That, at any rate, was what the court followers in Moscow and in foreign ministries abroad believed, racing to be the first to decipher Baranov's hidden meaning.

The pseudonym he used for these pronouncements, Nikolai Brandeis, added a further element of confusion. Adepts quickly recognized it as the name of a minor character in a seldom-read novel by Joseph Roth. Brandeis, a Tatar, plays the part of deus ex machina, appearing at crucial moments in the story only to disappear immediately after. "It doesn't require strength to conquer something," he says. "Everything yields to you, everything's rotten and surrenders. Knowing how to give things up, that's what counts." Just as the other characters in Roth's novel track Nikolai Brandeis's actions obsessively, since his extraordinary indifference is the only guarantor of success, so the high-ranking officeholders in the Kremlin and their satellites would pounce on the slightest indication of Baranov's thinking, in the hope of learning the tsar's intentions. What made the whole exercise precarious was that the Wizard of the Kremlin believed that plagiarism was the foundation of all progress. You could therefore never truly tell whether he was expressing his own ideas or playing with someone else's.

This game of cat and mouse reached its high point one winter night, when a dense pack of luxury cars, with their escort of sirens and bodyguards, converged on a small avant-garde theater in Moscow where a one-act play by a certain Nikolai Brandeis was being performed. Queueing at the door were bankers, oil magnates, ministers, and FSB generals. "In a civilized country," says the play's central character, "civil war would erupt, but as we don't have citizens here, we'll have a war between lackeys. It's no worse than a civil war, just a bit more distasteful, more sordid." To all appearances, Baranov wasn't in the crowd that night, but to be safe the bankers and ministers still applauded wildly. Some claimed that Baranov was watching the audience through a tiny peephole to the right of the balcony.

Yet even these somewhat childish games hadn't cured Baranov of his disaffection. At a certain point, the few people who actually met with him began to notice that his moods were growing darker. He was reported to be anxious, tired. Thinking of other things. He'd climbed the ranks too soon, and now he was bored, with himself most of all. And with the tsar, who for his part was never bored. And who was starting to hate Baranov. What? I brought you all this way and you have the gall to be bored? One should never under-estimate the sentimental side of political relationships.

Until one day Baranov disappeared. A terse note from the Kremlin announced that the political advisor to the president of the Russian Federation had resigned. And then all trace of him disappeared, except for occa-sional sightings of him around the globe, though none were ever confirmed.

When I arrived in Moscow a few years later, Baranov's memory hovered in the air like an amorphous shadow. No longer tied to his quite-substantial physical body, it was free to appear in one place or another, wherever it could be used to explain a particularly obscure action on the part of the Kremlin. And given that Moscow—inscrutable capital of a new era whose contours none could define—had come unexpectedly into the forefront once again, obsessive interpreters of the former magus of the Kremlin had cropped up even among those of us in the foreign community. A BBC journalist had made a documentary arguing that Baranov was the man responsible for bringing the techniques of avant-garde theater into politics. Another journalist described him in a book as a kind of magician who made people and political parties appear and disappear at the snap of his fingers. A professor had devoted a scholarly monograph to him: *Vadim Baranov and the Invention of Fake Democracy*. Everyone wanted to know what he had been up to recently. Did he still have influence over the tsar? What role had he played in the war in Ukraine? And what was his contribution to the propaganda strategy that had worked such profound changes on the planet's geopolitical equilibrium?

I personally followed these lines of inquiry with a certain detachment. The living have never interested me as much as the dead. I'd felt unmoored in the world until I realized that I could spend the better part of my time with the dead. Which is why my stay in Moscow was mostly spent visiting libraries and archives, along with a few restaurants, and a café where the waiters gradually became accustomed to my solitary presence. I pored over old books, took walks in the pale winter light, and in the late afternoons went to the steam baths on Seleznevskaya Street to be restored. At night, a small bar in Kitay-gorod warmly enclosed me behind its doors of rest and forgetfulness. And at almost every point, there walked at my side a marvelous phantom, a potential ally.

To all intents and purposes, Yevgeny Zamyatin appears to be an early twentieth-century writer, born in a village of Romani and horse thieves, who was arrested and sent into exile by the tsarist authorities for taking part in the 1905 revolution. Admired early on for his fiction, he worked as a naval engineer in England, where he manufactured icebreakers. He then returned to Russia in 1917 to join the Bolshevik Revolution, but quickly realized that building a paradise for the working class was not on the agenda. And so Zamyatin began to write a novel, *We*. And at that point, something happened that helps us understand what physicists mean when they talk of parallel universes.

In 1922, Zamyatin stopped being just a writer and became a time machine. He thought he was writing a biting criticism of the Soviet system as it was then being built. That's certainly how the censors read *We*, and it's on that basis that they stopped its publication. But the truth is that Zamyatin was not addressing them. Without realizing it, he had stepped into the next century and was speaking directly to our era. *We* depicts a society governed by logic, where everything has a number, and where each person's life is regulated down to the tiniest detail for maximum efficiency. The result is a rigid but comfortable dictatorship, one in which anyone can compose three sonatas in an hour by pushing a button, and where relations between the sexes are automatically regulated through a mechanism that selects the most-compatible partners and allows copulation with each of them. Everything is transparent in Zamyatin's world, down to a membrane in the street, decorated as a work of art, that records the conversation of passersby. Clearly, this is a place where voting also has to be public. "The ancients are said to have voted secretly, furtively, like thieves," says the main character, named D-503. "What was the point of all this mystery? It's never been fully determined... We don't hide anything, we aren't ashamed of anything. We celebrate our elections openly, loyally, and in the full light of day. I watch everyone else vote for the Benefactor, and everyone else watches me vote for the Benefactor."

I'd been obsessed with Zamyatin ever since discovering him. His work seemed to concentrate all the questions of our times. *We* didn't describe the Soviet Union. It was about our own smooth, seamless, algorithm-driven world, the global matrix presently under construction, and the total inadequacy of our primitive brains to deal with it. Zamyatin was an oracle. He was not just speaking to Stalin, he was targeting all the dictators waiting in the wings, the oligarchs of Silicon Valley as well as the mandarins of China's single political party. His book was the last weapon against the digital beehive that was starting to enmesh the planet. My task was to dig it up again and point it in the right direction. The problem was that I didn't exactly have the means at hand to make Mark Zuckerberg or Xi Jinping tremble, but I did manage to talk my university into financing my research into Zamyatin's life, by pointing to the fact that he had spent his last years in Paris after escaping Stalin. A French publisher had expressed a vague interest in re-issuing *We*, and a friend who produced documentaries had been willing to consider the possibility of a project involving Zamyatin. "Try to find some material while you're in Moscow," he'd said, sipping a negroni at a ninth-arrondissement bar.

But I'd no sooner arrived in Moscow than I was distracted from my task, discovering that this pitiless city held its share of enchantments, tempting me to venture out every day into the narrow, frozen streets of Petrova and the Arbat. The moroseness of the blank Stalinist facades was tempered by the pale reflections of the old boyar residences, and even the snow, pounded to mud by the constant passing of black town cars, became pure again in the courtyards and small hidden gardens, which murmured their tales of times past.

These different timelines—the 1920s of Zamyatin and the dystopian future of *We*, the scars Stalin had left on the city and the more benign traces of prerevolutionary Moscow—all converged in me, producing a temporal dislocation that became my normal state of being. Still, I wasn't completely uninterested in what was happening around me. I'd stopped reading the newspapers by then, but my limited need for information was amply supplied by social media.

Among the Russian accounts that I followed was one that went by the name of Nikolai Brandeis. It was probably a student in some studio apartment in Kazan, rather than the actual Wizard of the Kremlin, but I read his posts without knowing for certain. No one knows anything in Russia, and either you cope or you leave. It was no great commitment, because Brandeis only posted a sentence every week or two. These never commented on the news, tending instead to hide a literary reference, or quote the lyrics of a song, or allude to a piece in the *Paris Review*, all of which supported the hypothesis of the student in Kazan.

"All is allowed in paradise, except for curiosity."

"If your friend dies, don't bury him. Stand by and wait. The vultures will gather soon, and you'll have many new friends."

"There is nothing sadder in this world than to watch a strong, healthy family reduced to shreds by a stupid banality. A pack of wolves, for instance."

The young man had a fairly dark turn of mind, but it fit in well enough with the local character.

One night, instead of going to my usual bar, I decided to stay home and read. I was renting two rooms on the top floor of a handsome building from the 1950s, built by German prisoners of war—a mark of standing in Moscow, where power and bourgeois comfort always rest on a solid foundation of oppression. Snow squalls lashed the window, muting the orange glow of the city beyond. Inside, the apartment had an air of improvisation that seems to follow me wherever I go: stacks of books and a scattering of fast-food cartons and half-empty bottles of wine. Marlene Dietrich's voice layered a touch of decadence over the scene, reinforcing the sense of strangeness that at the time gave me great pleasure.

I'd set Zamyatin aside for a Nabokov short story, but his work was quietly putting me to sleep, as it often did. The writer in residence at the Montreux Palace had always been a little too highbrow for my taste. My eyes would wander from the page every few minutes, unconsciously looking for sustenance, and inevitably be drawn to my computer tablet. There, among the trending expressions of outrage and the koala bear pictures, this sentence suddenly leaped out: "We live surrounded by transparent walls that seem to be knitted of sparkling air; we live beneath the eyes of everyone, always bathed in light." Zamyatin. Seeing it materialize in my news feed hit me like a sledgehammer. Almost automatically, I added these words from *We* to Brandeis's tweet: "Besides, this makes much easier the burdensome and noble task of the Guardians, for who knows what might happen otherwise?"

Then I threw my tablet across the room to return to reading. The next morning, when I fished the device from under the cushions, the blasted thing was flashing at me to check my messages. "I didn't know that people still read Z." It was from Brandeis, writing at three in the morning. I answered without thinking: "Z is the hidden king of our times." And a question came back, "How long will you be in Moscow?"

I hesitated for a moment. How did this student know where I was? Then I realized that the tweets I'd posted in the last few weeks had probably let slip that I was in Moscow, maybe with a little reading between the lines. I answered that I didn't know exactly, then went out into the frozen city to perform the daily rituals of my solitary existence. A new message was awaiting me on my return: "If you're still interested in Z, I have something to show you."

Why not? I had nothing to lose. At worst I'd make the acquaintance of a student with a passion for literature. Possibly a touch lugubrious at times, but that could generally be fixed with a glass or two of vodka.

2

THE CAR WAS WAITING at the curb, its motor idling. A new, black Mercedes—the basic unit of Moscow locomotion. Two hefty men stood smoking quietly beside it. Seeing me approach, one of them opened the rear door for me, then took his place beside the driver.

I made no attempt at conversation. Experience had taught me that I would draw nothing but monosyllables from my two minders. Locally, they're called postage stamps, because they have to stick to their charges. These are men who talk little, convey a sense of calm. Once a week they dine with their moms, bring them flowers and a box of chocolates. They pat the blond heads of children when the occasion presents. Some collect wine corks, or else they polish their motorcycles religiously. The most peaceful people in the world. Except on the rare occasions when they're not. Then it's a different story—and you're better off being someplace else.

Glimpses of the beloved city flashed past. Moscow. The saddest and loveliest of imperial capitals. Then an endless dark forest appeared, linked in my mind to the forests that extend unbroken to Siberia. I hadn't the slightest idea where we were. My telephone had stopped working when I climbed into the car. And the GPS stubbornly maintained our position at the opposite end of the city.

At a certain point, we turned off the main road and onto a track plunging into the forest. The car slowed very little, attacking the forest trail with the same vehemence it had previously shown on the highway. Let no one say that Russian drivers allow stupid banalities to intimidate them—a pack of wolves, for instance. We continued driving into the dark, not for terribly long, but long enough for somber premonitions to surface. The amused curiosity I'd felt till then gradually gave way to apprehension. In Russia, I told myself, things generally go very well, but when things go bad they go really bad. In Paris, the worst you have to fear is an overhyped restaurant, a contemptuous look from a pretty girl, or a traffic fine. In Moscow, the range of unpleasant experiences is considerably greater.

We came to a gate. From inside the sentry box, a guard waved us on. The Mercedes finally started driving more conservatively. Through the birch trees, a small lake appeared with swans floating on its surface like question marks in the night. After a final turn, the car pulled to a stop in front of a large white-and-yellow neoclassical structure.

I got out of the car and found myself before a Hamburg townhouse, tucked alongside Alster Lake, rather than an oligarch's mansion. It was the home of an old-school professional, a physician or a banker, in any case a strict Calvinist, devoted to his work and not given to ostentation. At the entrance, the hesitant figure of an elderly butler in corduroys made a striking contrast with the two thugs who had driven me here. If they belonged unequivocally to the bright and cruel city we had just left, this slightly stooped valet seemed to have been chosen by his employer to preside over an older, more private world.

Once through the door, I discovered a paneled entrance hall. Again, no concession had been made to the contemporary style so much in vogue elsewhere. Instead, as I followed my fragile Charon through a series of rooms, I saw a profusion of veneered furniture and lighted candelabra, gilt frames and Chinese rugs, all of which created a warm atmosphere, to which the frosted windowpanes and big, tile-decorated chimneypieces added. The impression of stern harmony that had met me at the threshold grew stronger from room to room, until we arrived at a study, where the butler ushered me to a small, formal divan straight from the waiting room of a character in *War and Peace.* On the opposite wall, the oil portrait of an older man, dressed as a court jester, eyed me mockingly.

I looked around, delighted and a little surprised. Luxury often has a distracting effect, but here it gave a sense of strength and concentration.

—You expected gold faucets, maybe?

Baranov was smiling. He spoke without sarcasm, seeming instead to be at ease, a man accustomed to taking possession of other people's thoughts. He had materialized without warning, probably through a side door. He wore a dark, lightweight jacket, supple and expensive. I stuttered an answer, but the Russian paid no attention.

—I apologize for the late hour, a bad habit that I've fallen into and now can't shake.

—You're not alone in following that pattern, I said, thinking of the gaiety of Moscow nightlife, and then realizing it could sound like a reference to the tsar's nocturnal habits.

A fleeting thought seemed to move across his heavy gaze.

—At any rate, I went on, it's a true pleasure to be here. What a magnificent place.

I'd barely spoken these words when I felt Baranov's eyes come to rest on me for the first time: Have you come all this way to bore me like the rest?

The Russian continued to stand.

—So you've read Zamyatin, he said, walking toward the door through which he'd entered. Come, I've something to show you.

We entered a room whose walls held a library fit for a Benedictine monastery. Thousands of ancient volumes gleamed on the bookshelves, reflecting the bright glow from an imposing stone fireplace.

—I didn't know you collected old books, I said, extending my record for stating the obvious.

—I don't collect them, he said. I read them. Two very different things.

The Russian appeared irritated. Collectors are little men, obsessed with a control they'll never have. Baranov didn't consider himself one of them.

—Actually, the books are not all mine, he said. Many of them I inherited from my grandfather.

I barely managed to hide my surprise. In the Soviet Union, handing down a library of old books through the family was not a normal occurrence.

—This, however, is something that I found, said Baranov, still not disposed to explanation. He fished a few handwritten pages from a leather briefcase. Take a look, he said, handing me the yellowed sheets.

It was a letter in Cyrillic characters, dated Moscow, June 15, 1931. I started to read.

Dear Iosif Vissarionovich,
The author of the present letter, condemned to the highest penalty, appeals to you with the request for the substitution of this penalty by another. My name is probably known to you.

> To me as a writer, being deprived of the op-
> portunity to write is nothing less than a death
> sentence.

I looked up. Baranov made a show of scrutinizing his book, giving me time to gather my wits.

—It's the original letter Zamyatin wrote to Stalin, he said, not looking around. When he requested autho-rization to leave the USSR.

I continued staring at Baranov for a long moment after hearing his explanation. I couldn't believe what I held in my hands. Then I found the strength to keep reading.

> I have no intention of presenting myself as
> a picture of injured innocence. I know that
> I have a highly inconvenient habit of speak-
> ing what I consider to be the truth rather than
> saying what may be expedient at the moment.
> Specifically, I have never concealed my attitude
> toward literary servility, fawning, and chame-
> leon changes of color: I have felt and still feel
> that this is equally degrading both to the writer
> and to the revolution.

I remained deep in the letter for a time. When I raised my eyes, Baranov was observing me.

—It's among the best letters of entreaty ever sent to Stalin by an artist, he said. Zamyatin never abases himself. He speaks straight out, as an ex-Bolshevik. He'd fought against the tsar's soldiers, he'd survived exile, he'd returned to join the revolution. The one problem was that he understood it all too quickly and was foolish enough to say so in writing.

Fresh from my communion with the author, I felt a duty to interject, uttering a number of platitudes on the implacable tension between art and power, on Zamyatin's nomadic nature, and on his belief that even a revolutionary idea, once it wins out, inevitably starts to become bourgeois. Baranov considered me with the amiable air of a family friend dragged to an end-of-year school event. When he saw that I'd exhausted my subject, he spoke again.

—Yes, that's all true enough. But I think something else is happening here as well. Zamyatin tried to stop Stalin, he understood that Stalin wasn't a politician but an artist. That the future would be determined not by the competition between two political programs but between two artistic visions. In the 1920s, Zamyatin and Stalin were two avant-garde artists vying for supremacy. The forces on either side were disproportionate, of course, as Stalin's medium was the flesh and blood of his people, his canvas a vast nation, and his public the inhabitants of an entire planet, who spoke his name with reverence in hundreds of languages. What the poet brings to life in imagination, the world-builder enacts on the stage of global history. Zamyatin fought the battle in near-complete isolation, yet he tried to resist the new order. He knew that Stalin's art would inevitably lead to the concentration camp—if you were going to regulate the life of the New Man, there could be no room for heresy. Which is why, although an engineer, Zamyatin turned to the weapons of literature, theater, and music. He understood that from the moment state power was used to crush dissonance, the gulag would follow as a matter of course. If illicit harmonies are suppressed, soon there will be nothing but marches in double time. The minor key, no longer compatible with the ideals of the new society, will become a class enemy. Major! Nothing but major! All roads lead to major! Music, even instrumental music, will be subservient to words. And no more symphonies will be composed unless they glorify Marxism-Leninism.

As he spoke these last words, a trace of emotion entered Baranov's voice, as though he were not just analyzing a historical event.

—When Zamyatin convinced his friend Shostakovich to compose *Lady Macbeth of Mtsensk*, he went on, it was because he knew that the future of the USSR depended on this portrayal. That the only way to get away from show trials and political purges was to reintroduce the individual who rebels against planned order. And when Stalin stood up, furious, and marched out of the Bolshoi after the third act, it was because he knew that the freedom of the composer and his characters was a direct challenge to his own power, his global art project. That's why he commissioned the infamous editorial in *Pravda* denouncing the composer for paying too much attention to his characters' broad sensuality and "bestial" behavior. In the Stalin project, there was room for the bestial instincts of only one person. Lenin's admonition that "It's necessary to dream" was followed to the letter, but only Stalin's dream was allowed; all others had to be suppressed.

Baranov paused. The comfortable room around us offered a striking contrast to the harsh world he was describing.

—When you think of it, he continued, the first half of the twentieth century was just that: a titanic confrontation between artists. Stalin, Hitler, Churchill. After them came the bureaucrats, because the world needed a rest. But today the artists are back. Look around you. Wherever you look, there is nothing but avant-garde artists who, instead of depicting reality, are busy creating it. Their style is the only thing that has changed. Today, instead of the artists of yesteryear, we have reality-show personalities. But the principle is the same.

—Are you one of them? I asked.

—Of course not, he said. I played at being an aide for a while. And now I'm retired.

—You don't miss the adrenaline?

—You know, the biggest wager you'll ever face is to wake up, drink your morning coffee, and take your daughter to school. Seriously, I think I've only really wanted something three or four times in my life. But when I have, I've usually managed to get it. And what I want now, I can assure you, is nothing more than this.

Baranov gestured toward the library around us, the old wooden globe, and the fire burning in the fireplace.

—What did the others in the Kremlin have to say about that?

—How do you think they reacted? said Baranov. Badly, of course. Within the aquarium, all is forgiven, whether you're a robber, an assassin, or a traitor. Desertion is different. What! You don't want something we'd kill for? The courtiers can never forgive you for it.

—And the tsar?

—The tsar is another story. He sees and forgives everything, said Baranov, an ironic gleam momentarily appearing in his eyes.

—Are you writing your memoirs?

—That's the last thing I would ever do.

—You'd have plenty to tell...

—No book, he said, will ever measure up to the actual exercise of power.

—The opposite argument could also be made, I countered.

A faint shadow flickered across his face. Baranov smiled.

"You're right," he said. "Let me reformulate. No book that I could write would ever measure up to the exercise of power."

—And what do you see power as being?

—You're asking too direct a question, he said. Power is like the sun, like death: you can't look at it head-on. Especially in Russia. But since you've come all this way, and if you have some time, I'd like to tell you a story.

Baranov stood and poured two glasses of whiskey from a crystal decanter. He handed me one and resumed his place in his leather armchair. For a moment he eyed me piercingly, then looked down at his glass.

—My grandfather, he said slowly, was a remarkable hunter.

3

—MY GRANDFATHER WAS A remarkable hunter. At home, he never put on his bathrobe without a servant to help him, but when it came to killing a wolf, he'd spend whole nights in the forest under the stars. Before the revolution, it was just a pastime. He'd studied law, and any career he might have wanted in the tsar's bureaucracy was open to him. But when the Bolsheviks took over, all he had left was hunting. In fact, the Bolsheviks gave him his freedom, though he would never have admitted it. He hated the Communists. He named his dogs after party leaders: "Here, Molotov!" and "Sit, Beria!" Luckily, he lived in relative isolation, and no one ever denounced him for it. But my father, even in childhood, knew how extravagant a man Grandfather was. He was ashamed of him. And terrified as well, I think. He wasn't wrong to feel that way, given all that was happening at the time. But Grandfather couldn't have cared less. Besides, things were going well for him. At a certain point, he started writing books on hunting: how to train dogs, identify tracks, that kind of thing. He would mix in a few anecdotes, describe some of the characters he met while in the field, quote passages from Turgenev—readers loved it. His books offered some of the lightheartedness of earlier times, but confined to a limited domain, which made them palatable to those in power. Eventually, Grandfather became something of an authority. In 1954, when wolves were spreading into the Caucasus, he was put in charge of a government expedition to exterminate them. He was practically a public official, but he never changed his attitude. He kept the characteristic insolence of the Russian aristocracy and could never resist making a witticism, even if he had to hang for it.

I remember him mocking my father when I was little: "Nice work, Alyosha, next thing Brezhnev will have you sitting on his lap during the Victory Day parade!" And: "You do know that the party has two kinds of functionaries, right?"

"Yes, Father, you've told me before."

"The good-for-nothings and the stop-at-nothings. So which are you, Alyosha?"

My dad shuddered. His disposition was the exact opposite. From childhood on, he'd tried hard to stay out of trouble. At the first opportunity, he joined the Young Pioneers, then the Komsomol. I think he hoped to atone for his eccentric father and his aristocratic heritage. He wanted to be like everyone else. I understand that. It's a form of rebellion in its own right. When you grow up with a parent so entirely outside the bounds of normality, the only way you can rebel is through conformity.

At any rate, I was sent every summer to stay with my grandfather in the country. The *isba* where he lived, a kind of log cabin made of poplar trunks, was just outside the village. Its exterior was rustic, and it stood in the middle of a kitchen garden with cucumbers, potatoes, bay laurel, and a few apple trees. There was also a small table with a set of cast-iron chairs so rusty they might have spent a century or two at the bottom of the Neva. But when you entered the house, you realized that Grandfather had somehow managed to re-create the atmosphere of an earlier age there. The small living room and the dining room weren't luxuriously furnished, but a sense of quiet prosperity hung in the air—completely at odds with the times—and the smell of tea always on the boil. There were plenty of hunting trophies and animal furs, but the master of the house had softened their presence by delicately interspersing them with more-unexpected objects: Chinese statuettes, a bezoar stone, and a few books with elaborate bindings scattered carelessly on the birch-wood table. The arrangement was graceful in what I would normally call a feminine way, were it not that my grandfather hated even the idea of cohabiting with the other sex. His wife, my father's mother, had died of peritonitis at the age of twenty-three, closing the chapter on his romantic life. A few female friends came to visit him from time to time, some more presentable than others. But none lingered more than a few hours in this temple to the gods of literature, the hunt, and virile friendship, fueled mostly by sarcastic repartee and bouts of heavy drinking.

The house was looked after by Zakhar and Nina, a peasant couple who officially worked at the kolkhoz but were in fact domestic servants. Grandfather was a superb horseman, but he'd never learned to drive a car. When he had to go somewhere, Zakhar would bring out the ancient Volga and chauffeur him. My grandfather's one concession to prudence was to sit democratically beside Zakhar rather than in the back seat. It always made for an adventure to accompany Grandfather, even if he was only going to the village on an errand. Things would happen there that happened to no one but him, as though he were wrapped in a nostalgic aura that protected him from the meanness of the times, thus allowing at any moment for an impromptu celebration. He could walk into the drabbest state café, and a spark of magic from the old days would suddenly flicker to life. Even when he was seated in a plastic chair on a gray linoleum floor, something about him brought forth images of formal balls, of slicing champagne bottles open with a saber. People, often complete strangers, sensed his charisma and were drawn by it, gathering around to hear this ever-courteous, elegant old gentleman tell stories of an earlier age as though he were attending a fashionable salon in Petersburg. Sometimes I'd notice an ill-tempered apparatchik glaring at him from a nearby table, but no one ever dared interfere with him. How Grandfather survived the Stalinist purges isn't clear, but with time the regime gradually shed its more carnivorous tendencies. Grandfather was just someone you had to put up with, and anyway he showed no interest in politics.

His friends were mostly hunters. A motley group, they included former aristocrats like him, but also peasants and Siberian brigands. There were even a few of what he called domesticated Communists, party members he'd managed to corrupt with his nostalgic talk and drinking sprees. In early winter, they would scatter vodka bottles around the *isba*'s grounds for the pleasure of finding them again when the snows melted. Meanwhile they would huddle indoors, congregating at least twice a week for cards. They swapped hunting stories and critiqued the current state of affairs, mostly by telling jokes.

"Do you know what a Soviet duo is? A quartet that's been touring abroad."

"Some government inspectors are visiting a psychiatric hospital. The patients line up to sing them a song: 'How Lovely to Live in the Soviet Union!' But the inspectors notice that one man is keeping quiet. 'Why

aren't you singing?' they ask. 'I'm one of the orderlies,'
he says, 'I'm not crazy!'"

"Comrade Khrushchev goes to visit a pig farm,
along with a photographer from *Pravda*. Later, in the
newsroom, the layout team is trying to decide how to
word the caption. Should it be 'Comrade Khrushchev
next to pigs,' or 'Comrade Khrushchev surrounded by
pigs,' or maybe 'Pigs gather around Comrade Khrushchev'? The suggestions are rejected one after another.
Finally, the editor steps in. 'OK, here it is,' he says.
'Comrade Khrushchev, third from right.'"

There was hilarity at these gatherings, hearty
thumps on the back, and the draining of decanter after
decanter. Yet Grandfather's house was not always pul-
sating with activity. He liked being alone. He said it was
because he didn't care for Communists, but the truth is
that he'd have been a misanthrope under any regime. I
think I've inherited some of his characteristics...

Baranov smiled. He reached for the bottle and poured
a shot of whiskey into his crystal glass.

—Sitting by the fireplace one night, Grandfather started
to tell me stories about the tsar's troops in Paris after
Napoleon's defeat. A recurrent figure in these stories
was a man called Yurko, an inveterate drinker and a

brother-in-arms of an ancestor of ours who served in
the imperial guard. On Yurko's arrival in Paris, he ran
into a pharmacy, grabbed a bottle of medical alcohol,
sniffed it, and poured it down his throat, following it
with two small cucumbers he had brought especially
for the occasion. The pharmacist panicked, already
imagining the firing squad he would face for poison-
ing a Russian soldier. He rushed to the nearest encamp-
ment, where he stopped the first more or less civilized
Russian officer he met. This turned out to be Vassily
Baranov. The pharmacist explained that he'd had no
hand in Yurko's impending death, that the Russian had
downed the bottle before he could say a word. Our
ancestor interrupted him at this point. "You've had
little acquaintance with Russian soldiers, I believe?"
The pharmacist agreed. "But you're familiar with the
concept of immunity, no?" The pharmacist stared, bewildered. "Look here, dear sir, life in Russia is full of
hardships, exceeding anything you have in Paris. Our
choice of cheeses is very limited, our women hardly
ever smile, and our roads are almost always glazed with
ice. But what doesn't kill you makes you stronger: over
the centuries, our metabolisms have had a chance to
adapt to many things." He then pointed to Yurko, who
was quietly playing at cards with two comrades, a half-
empty bottle of vodka on the table between them.

Grandfather burst out laughing and went on:
"When I was eighteen, I, too, was accepted into the
tsar's guard. I was very proud of it, but it had little

to do with my merits, as you're aware. My father and grandfather served in the same regiment before me, and, for all I know, every Baranov before them served there as well. At any rate, I was proud as anything and received congratulations from all sides: "What a tremendous privilege, Kolya, to serve in the tsar's guard, what good fortune for your parents," et cetera, et cetera. Then one day, during our morning exercises, I fell from my horse and broke my pelvis. My friends all said, "Bad luck, Kolya, the social season is starting and the first balls are just being announced!" I was desperate. My regimental brethren were strutting around in their dress uniforms at one dazzling gala after another, while I was in bed playing cards with my babushka. But suddenly, war broke out, and they left for the front. Poor fellows, they were all mowed down by German machine guns on their first charge. I was still convalescing at home, visited by a strong feeling of guilt, of course, but also by the many young beauties of Petersburg who came to console me.

"It was then that I met your grandmother. Times were hard, but we had great expectations, or so we thought. My family's high rank and the law studies I'd embarked on opened the door for me to work in the highest tiers of the administration. I began to be received at court, and my father-in-law started building a small palace on Nevsky Prospect. Our path seemed laid out once and for all, when a bunch of nitwits suddenly decided the tsar had to be ousted and our Holy Mother

Russia turned into a republic. They pulled it off, too, and took power! But then the Bolsheviks swooped in and massacred everyone, tsarists and republicans alike.

"The revolution was an unprecedented catastrophe. But it's true that without it, I'd have ended up a functionary, or at best a courtier. I'll never say that Communism is a good thing, but the truth is that you can be happy whatever regime is in power. And do you know what, Vadya? You never know anything. You can't control what happens, and, even worse, you can't tell if what does happen is good or bad. You're there, you're expecting something, you want it to come about with all your might. It finally does, and instantly you realize that your life is ruined. Or else the opposite. The sky falls on your head, but you gradually recognize that you could not have hoped for a better outcome. All you can control, believe me, is how you interpret the events that do happen. If you start from the idea that it's not things but the way we interpret them that make us suffer, then you have a chance of taking control of your life. Otherwise, you're doomed to blast at flies with a cannon."

I still remember my grandfather's expression as he said these words. He spoke seriously, but also with a touch of irony, as though he were a little embarrassed to play the part of the tedious old codger. But he wanted to do it. Men of that generation wanted to pass on what they'd learned about life, they felt it was important. I think they were the last to have had this feeling. Starting with my father's generation, people stopped believing there was any point in transmitting anything at all. We've become too *cool*, too modern. And we live in fear of ridicule. No one wants to play the old fool.

My grandfather was not a nineteenth-century patriarch, he was a modern man. He'd read Kafka and Thomas Mann, but he was willing to risk ridicule to tell me what he had to say. And I'll always be grateful to him for it, because the idea has stayed with me ever since that we are groping in the dark. That we know neither what's good for us nor what's bad. But that we're free to decide on the meaning of the things that do happen. And that's our one and only strength.

4

—WHO KNOWS HOW GRANDFATHER managed to keep the family library hidden? I think no one ever dared to search through his possessions. Even we were not allowed to visit the attic. From time to time he would come down from there carrying a book. "Here, these are Casanova's *Memoirs*. But don't tell your father." At first it was mostly children's books: La Fontaine's *Fables*, or a novel by the Comtesse de Ségur. Then he grew impatient. He wanted to have someone to discuss books with, even if it was only a child. So he started bringing down works of a different sort. I was not yet ten, I believe, when he handed me the *Memoirs* of the Cardinal of Retz, which I read as a cloak-and-dagger story. At that stage, I was more familiar with Louis de Bourbon and the Duchess of Longueville than with Mickey Mouse or Misha the Bear.

———

Baranov smiled and gestured toward a section of his library.

—A good portion of these books were his. And almost all of them are in French, as you can see. The peak of civilization, Grandfather used to say. The world in which he came of age modeled itself on Paris, copying its manners, its fashions, and its quirks to the point of absurdity. Did you know that Nesselrode, the celebrated Russian negotiator at the Congress of Vienna, spoke no Russian? For forty years, he directed foreign policy for the Russian Empire, yet he didn't speak our language. All that love and passion, directed not at being oneself but someone else! And how was this great love repaid? With contempt. Always and in every age, the same contempt!

—Take that son of a bitch Custine, the so-called Tocqueville of Russia, said Baranov, reaching for another book. Tsar Nicholas treated him like a brother, received him at court, upended protocol so Custine could attend his daughter's wedding, and how did the son of a bitch pay him back? He wrote four volumes, thirteen hundred pages, describing Russia as pure hell. Listen: "This empire, immense as it is, is no more than a prison, of which the emperor keeps the key. And though he may be its jailer, the jailers live little better than the prisoners." Or this, "The Russians have less interest in being civilized than in persuading others to believe that they are."

Grandfather hated *Russia in 1839*. But it fascinated him. "That damn Frenchman is the best interpreter of Russia," he would say, "because in this country the court provides the only path to power and wealth. Relying on popular sentiment here does you no good. The winner is always the one whose power base is at court. Which is why adulation is more effective than talent, and silence than eloquence. Custine watched the noblemen of St. Petersburg walk outdoors in winter without coats, so great was their adulation of the tsar. And they died. There were no cafés in which to discuss the daily newspaper, and, of course, there were no newspapers. The news was as varied as the person passing it on, usually in hushed tones. Russia is a country of mutes, a Sleeping Beauty country, lovely but lifeless because the breath of freedom is missing. Today as much as yesterday."

When Grandfather spoke like this, my father shook with terror. He was afraid of the library in the attic, which he considered a potentially subversive place. But to his lasting credit, he never forced the issue and barred me from it. Not that he was at home that often. He was always traveling somewhere to give a speech or attend a symposium. At a certain point he was named director of the Communist Party's Academy of Social

Science, and his name was listed in the *Great Soviet Encyclopedia*, the ultimate honor at the time. But he was always a cautious man, basically. I think his main objective was to never wake up with the secret police banging on his door. You have no idea how much talent has been sacrificed in Russia on the altar of this one goal.

—It strikes me as proof of his common sense, I said.

—Maybe. My father had his share of common sense, no question. But when I think back on it, it struck me even then as a kind of catastrophic naivete—to think that you could fulfill your duty, that a man who jumped into the vortex of duties could come to the end of them someday. If you looked closely at my father, he always seemed to be crushed under this burden, one that he himself had placed on his own shoulders. Grandfather called him "the little Red Guard." It made me laugh as a child, but I have to admit that it's only because of my father, because of his career and his cautious approach, that I was able to enjoy the many privileges that Soviet life afforded at the time—special shops that carried products imported from abroad; schools where they taught English, German, and French; reserved seats at the theater, though it was best not to attend too often, at the risk of being taken for an artist or a freethinker.

Back then, the most highly sought-after privilege was the *kremliovka*, the basket of provisions reserved for high functionaries and members of the party's Central Committee. Every day, my father's chauffeur, Vitali, went to Two Granovskovo Street to fetch our *krem-liovka*. And whenever I could get permission, I went with him. The chauffeur stopped in front of what appeared to be a store like any other, but you knew something was going on inside because there were almost always official cars parked out front, their motors running. Vitali and I would enter the building and walk down a long hallway to a glass door, with a sign saying "Permit Office." Vitali would knock and enter without waiting for a response. Behind the counter was a woman, dressed in gray, who greeted him with a smile. This in itself was a rare privilege, because bureaucrats in the Soviet Union never smiled at you. She'd ask Vitali what she might get for him. He would turn to me and say, "So, Vladenka, what shall we eat today?" And I could choose whatever I liked: salmon piroshki and lamb chops, Lenov caramels and oranges from Azerbaijan. I don't think I've ever felt such a sense of well-being and absolute power since.

Baranov looked around him, as if to say that all this opulence, all this wood paneling and ceiling stucco, was nothing next to the basket of piroshki he'd eaten as a child.

—The problem, basically, is that I had a happy childhood. And it affected me, I think. I never felt the

slightest resentment, never needed to revenge myself
against the world, which is a serious handicap for a
person leading the kind of life I do. And it's not normal
in Russia. Here everyone remembers their earlier life,
their sacrifices. The Russian elite all share a common
origin in poverty, before they came into their villas on
the Côte d'Azur, their bottles of Pétrus. Some people
trumpet their start in life, others are ashamed of it, but
when they look at each other, wearing their thirty-
thousand-dollar suits, they know they share the same
rage, the same shock at how things have turned out.
Even the tsar. Despite being convinced of his destiny,
of the inexorable force that put him where he is, he
can't always hide an expression of disbelief. Me, the
kid from the *kommunalka* on Baskov Street, here I am
at Buckingham Palace, and the queen is serving me
tea! For me, however, it was different. At my house
there were servants in white gloves coming around
with trays of pink gin. True, there wasn't a great deal
of money. But back then you didn't need it.

—Unlike today.

—Right, unlike today. Though that's only partly
true. Foreigners think the new breed of Russian is obsessed with money. But that's not what it is. Russians
play with money. They shoot it into the air like fire-
works. It came so fast and in such torrents. Yesterday,
there was none. Tomorrow, who knows? You might as
well spend it all right away. In your country, money
is essential, it's the foundation of everything. Here, I

can tell you, that's not the case. The only thing that matters in Russia is privilege, proximity to power. Everything else is secondary. That's how things were in tsarist times, and in the Communist era even more so. The Soviet system was based on status. Money counted for nothing. There wasn't much in circulation, and it was useless in any case—no one ever thought to judge people on the basis of how much of it they had. If you went out and bought a dacha instead of waiting for the party to give you one—because that was something you could do, even back then—it was an admission that you might not be important enough to receive one as a gift. Status was what counted, not cash. And it was a trap, of course. Privilege is the antithesis of freedom, something like a form of slavery. Do you know what a *vertushka* is?

—No.

—A telephone. In the Communist era, it was what everyone coveted. Because it wasn't just any phone. It was a special piece of equipment that allowed you to call all the big shots in government. *Vertushka* numbers had only four digits. When they installed one in your office, it meant you'd arrived. Every year, a register was printed, with all the names in the *vertushka* network between red leather covers. If you were a registered user, you were required to dial the number yourself and answer incoming calls personally, no matter who was calling. If you were very high-ranking, you also got a *vertushka* at home, at the dacha, and in the car.

People who had them could make all their calls on the *vertushka*. Using an ordinary telephone was looked on as a sign of false modesty and as a failure to be grateful for the privilege you'd been granted. Something a free-thinker might do, and probably an act of subversion.

Baranov paused and half smiled.

—Of course, the KGB monitored all the conversations, but that didn't stop anyone. Strangely, what courtiers most want are the instruments of their own submission.

I understood this one night, entirely by accident. My father, who loved the movies, occasionally arranged a private screening at the academy. He'd invite a few colleagues and an official or two from the Central Committee, about ten people in all. The film had to be chosen carefully. You couldn't show just anything. But the normal censorship didn't apply to him, and my father could screen just about any movie he wanted. After all, he was the director of the academy, and if *he* didn't study the artifacts of Western bourgeois decadence, who would? In any case, when I was about twelve or thirteen, he showed *The Taking of Power by Louis XIV*, directed by Roberto Rossellini. Do you know the movie?

I nodded with the faintly guilty air of a person who has promised himself on several occasions to watch a film and never found the strength to do so.

—It's the story of the Sun King, who builds his palace at Versailles and obliges all the nobles to attend him there, and who then uses ceremonies and small privileges as a cage in which to constrain them. He takes away their freedom, almost without their noticing, and in many cases their fundamental dignity as well. In the final scene, we see the king strip off his ornaments and luxurious accessories. The sumptuous clothes were just an artifice, a tool for asserting power. They were meant, as he tells his minister, to make each person in his court depend for all things on the sovereign, just as nature depends for all things on the sun.

That night, when the lights came back on in the projection hall, I had the impression that the audience was uncomfortable. They weren't stupid people, far from it. They'd studied and received degrees, hoisted themselves to the apex of the pyramid at the cost of much effort, great sacrifice, and considerable scheming. But on this occasion, after seeing the movie, they looked around at each other strangely. Almost as if they were embarrassed, in a way they couldn't explain. They filed from the room a little faster than usual, and each drove home in the official car the party had put at their disposal around the clock.

The Soviet elite, in fact, had a great deal in common with the tsarist nobility. They were a little less elegant, maybe, and a little more educated, but with the same aristocratic contempt for money, the same sidereal distance from the people, the same propensity for arrogance and violence. You can't escape your fate, and Russia's fate is to be governed by the descendants of Ivan the Terrible. Invent whatever you like—the proletarian revolution, unbridled liberalism—but the result is always the same. At the top are the *oprichniki*, the tsar's guard dogs. At least today there is a modicum of order, a semblance of respect. That's already something. And we'll see how long it lasts.

Baranov stood up abruptly, as though unexpectedly struck by an idea, and moved toward his desk.

—*Vertushkas* still exist, did you know that? They're the FSB's secure landlines. Anyone who wants to talk with the tsar has to have one. Look, there it is.

Baranov pointed to an old-fashioned telephone at one corner of his desktop.

—I thought it would be red!
—No, he said. It's gray, like everything else.

—If you think Moscow is gray, you should come spend a few days in Europe. Or visit Washington.

—Not a chance! They aren't gray over there, they're dead.

He flashed a hard smile.

—As you know, he said, I'm no longer free to visit those places.

—Yes, I'd heard. Somewhere you said that the only things you missed from the United States were Tupac Shakur, Allen Ginsberg, and Jackson Pollock, but that you didn't need to go there to enjoy them.

—One says stupid things.

—What happened to your father?

—I told you. He was a nice man, meticulous, always busy composing a weighty tome on "The Dialectics of the Contemporary Era" or "The Theoretical Problems of Soviet Linguistics." And for a time that all went very well. At the age of fifty, he received the Lenin Prize, and all the libraries in the Soviet Union had to carry bound volumes of his work, which were printed in tens of thousands of copies. Then Gorbachev arrived with his glass of milk!

—His glass of milk?

—Yes. You could tell Gorbachev was going to destroy the Soviet Union just by looking at him—you didn't even have to listen. He would climb onto the dais, and someone would bring him a glass of milk. People couldn't believe their eyes. Next, he doubled the price of vodka. He wanted everyone to drink milk. In

Russia. Can you imagine? And people are surprised the country went down the drain.

At any rate, that was the end of it for my father. He lost everything—his job, his privileges, his literary honors. Everything he'd spent a half century building. The only thing they left him was the apartment, full of impenetrable books of Marxist criticism. But he was forced to sell that, too, in the end.

The worst of it was that all the tenets that his life was founded on collapsed at once. I was in high school at the time, but I wasn't a particularly enthusiastic student. I got by, and I found odd jobs to do. I bought television sets and tape recorders and resold them. Things like that. It wasn't long before I was earning more than my father. And people would turn up at the house asking for me, not him. I was sixteen and didn't know anything, but I was better adapted to the new world than he was, who knew it all.

Eventually he stopped leaving the house. Other relics of the Soviet era would drop by from time to time, but they all felt a sense of shame, even about their memories. So they would sit there in silence, like the ruined walls of an abandoned temple.

When he fell ill, it was almost a relief. "I finally have a good reason to stay in bed," he'd say. He lay there quietly, smoking his pipe and rereading the classics—Gogol, Pushkin, Tolstoy.

During this period, he was almost lighthearted, as though he'd been delivered of a great weight. It might

seem paradoxical, but illness is not necessarily a serious
state. Seriousness, application, hard work—these are
the prerogatives of people in good health. The dying
have nothing left to do, they can enjoy the passing
days. That was true for my father, at any rate. His
ambition finally took a nap, like a child after a play
session. He had time to stroll at Patriarch Ponds, to
warm himself in the sun, to read a book. And not the
kind of book he'd had to read for his lectures either,
but a beautiful and completely useless one. Eventually,
he had to be hospitalized, in the Kremlin clinic. It was
still a privilege, but times had changed, and the big star
on the ward, the person to whom all eyes were drawn,
was not him—a miserable shadow from the past. No,
the star was a large and vulgar woman who spoke with
a Saratov accent and prattled all day about her vacation
in Sardinia, her shopping trips to London, her soirees
in Monte Carlo. The nurses and the other patients were
riveted. They smiled idiotically at the descriptions of
private jets and saltwater swimming pools. And the
truth of everything the woman said was confirmed by
the jewels dangling at her throat and earlobes, by her
Cartier watch, and by the latest electronic gadgets she
so casually displayed. My father took it in his stride.
For the first time in his life he seemed completely uninterested in the world's opinion of him. It was as if his
proximity to death gave him a sense of control over his
life that he'd never had before. The doctors and nurses
went to great lengths to convince him that he wasn't

dying at all, that he'd be back to his old self within weeks. But he knew it wasn't true and derived a certain pride from it. "They're ashamed and they'd like to hide the truth from me. But I know that I'm about to die, and can I tell you something? I'm ready, much readier than I'd have ever thought."

As he approached the end of his life, it seemed that he stood tall for the first time and showed a degree of courage that even he hadn't known he possessed. The only real conversations we ever had came during this period. I sat on the right side of his bed in one of those nasty plastic hospital chairs, and we spent whole afternoons discussing history and philosophy, alongside trifling matters, our shared past, and Grandfather's French books, just as though we were in the country, sprawled on the leather armchairs at the *isba*, with the smell of birch logs drifting through the room. He spoke in a tone that I'd never heard him use before, caustic, biting, somewhat disenchanted. He was brilliant, and he had my grandfather's sense of irony. It didn't seem possible that he could have hidden this whole side of himself for so long. Suddenly, his career as a bureaucrat in the knowledge field seemed both tragic and absurd.

And then one day he died. The funeral was by no means a grand affair. Four unhappy souls followed the casket in a dented car, as the nouveaux riches in their Mercedes whisked past us at top speed.

It suddenly occurred to me that the man had basically lived his whole life so as to be given a fancy funeral. Eulogies, the respect of the people, a military salute, a floral wreath from the secretary-general of the party, a parade of dignitaries, and an obituary in *Pravda*. He got none of that. But even if he had, how would it have changed things? You have no idea how many people live that way. In order to be given a fancy funeral. Some are successful, others not. But what's the difference?

It's not what I want. I thought that then, and I think it now. So after my father's death, I looked at the course he'd charted for me, and went in the other direction.

5

WHEN YOU'RE YOUNG, IT'S not enough to do something, you also need to justify it. My father wanted me to become a diplomat. He pictured me in a drawing room in Vienna or Paris, happily dissecting Russian literature with a silver-haired ambassador. But what I wanted was to get away once and for all from the world of goals, duties, and plans. So I enrolled in the Moscow Academy of Theater Arts and started living the disorderly life of a drama student.

In the early 1990s, Moscow was an electric city. We'd just turned twenty, and a new world was opening up before us, right when we were finally strong enough to conquer it. The streets of Moscow, the giant Stalinist buildings, the muddy sidewalks, and the big ceiling lights in the Metro were all still the same, but everything suddenly seemed to exist within a bubble of energy. We were so excited that we never slept more than three or four hours a night. I remember my courses at the academy. For the first time we were attending Western performances, and we even got to meet the actors and directors, sometimes talking with them till dawn.

We were convinced that it was now our turn to remake society from the ground up, captives of the Russian notion that art is more than just culture, that it's prophecy, truth, and social construction. We came from a world of whispers and hushed speech, where the few who had the courage to speak openly were madmen or heroes. We hadn't yet realized that words counted for nothing, that only action counts. In those years, the periodicals that covered art and literature sold millions of copies. People couldn't believe that they could finally read all those words, free and unfiltered. Their appetite for them was endless. You can imagine how we felt, actually living the myth of art as redemption. Even I, at that point, pretended to believe in it. You know how the young are, they take everything so damn seriously. It's the curse of youth.

And then there was Ksenia. I'd met her at a party, one of those gatherings where at a certain point half the guests start punching each other, while the other half are making out in the bathrooms. In the middle of it all sat a stunning young woman, as still as if about to start a backgammon game in a quiet square on a Greek island.

I approached her with some excuse or other and embarked on a story I thought terribly amusing at the time. She smiled dreamily and said with cutting cruelty, "How absolutely fascinating! Do you have more stories in that vein?"

What was disconcerting up close was that she didn't have the slightest flaw, not even a beauty mark to detract from the perfect symmetry of her face, unless you counted the expression in her eyes, which glowed with an almost violet light.

"No, that was my best one!"

Her smile softened almost imperceptibly. Somehow, I'd made first contact with Planet Ksenia.

Her parents were both hippies. We had them here too, you know. Her mother was from Estonia, within range of Finnish television broadcasts, so the new fashions always reached them first. She met a musician at a concert near Smolensk; they clicked, and Ksenia was conceived. A love child, she was always told. Then the parents went their separate ways. Ksenia grew up trailing her mother, hitchhiking from place to place, from campsite to festival, from one school to another. People looked at them disapprovingly. They, in turn, took common sense as their enemy. The girl's only moments of stability came when her mother, wanting more freedom to pursue her fantasies, parked Ksenia with her grandparents. This upbringing left Ksenia with a strong sense of indifference, confirmed nomadic habits, and a bored tolerance for transgressions of every kind. She moved through her daily life as if skating on ice, striking sparks from it at times, as the common run of mortals never do. But because she only found release in highly charged situations, the most humdrum circumstances could drive her crazy. Despite her intelligence, she was too lazy and too distracted to follow a logical process, yet her blazing intuition sometimes led her to the heart of a problem that had baffled everyone else. At other times, she would become hopelessly entangled in a calculation that would seem obvious to a four-year-old. She had the knack of looking into a person's eyes and seeing everything that had happened to them, but she was so centered on herself that she quickly forgot, and it was then as though she'd seen nothing. Life as she understood it had nothing to do with pursuing a career or making plans, and she held that when men started talking about the future they automatically became boring. Her ideal was to spend the afternoon on a sofa reading and sleeping. But she sometimes exploded into a whirlwind of activity. She would organize huge parties or expeditions into the wilderness, stage a series of plays, or learn to speak Japanese. She was successful at everything she did because of her many talents, but she never put them to use for long.

I sometimes thought that even if I lived a thousand years, I would never meet another person like Ksenia. But living with her was not exactly easy. Whenever we'd been apart, even for a brief period, it would all have to start again from zero. Ksenia would scrutinize me for the slightest weakness—a lowering of the eyes, a trace of sweat on my forehead, the least hesitation in my voice. She was like a tigress, ready to pounce at the first sign of fear. Her eyes would still be smiling, while her lips were already quivering with rage. Then her eyes would change color. Usually gray, they would grow lighter and lighter until they turned almost white. It was the signal that a storm was about to break. Frantically, you'd review the events of the past hours to find a reason. Most of the time, you'd draw a blank, because the crisis could have been set off by almost anything—a fleeting impression, the recollection of something that had happened months earlier, or a momentary spasm of boredom.

The scenario was always the same. Ksenia, her eyes mere slits, would lash out at you savagely, spewing all the helpless rage that had built up in her since birth. How you reacted made no difference. If you held your peace, the torrent of insults would continue and swell, feeding on your passivity as the ultimate proof of your cowardice. If you reacted and tried to respond, or eventually lashed out in return, the result was the same. Ksenia used your words as material for further invective. Then, like a rainstorm, the rage would stop, and Ksenia would forget even what she'd just said. She'd notice you were upset and ask what the matter was. Sometimes she graced you with a hug. She needed to be consoled, a shattered child that nothing could ever fully reassure.

The terror Ksenia inspired owed largely to her un-predictability. Like great dictators throughout history, Ksenia instinctively knew that nothing inspires more fear than random punishment. If punishment can strike unexpectedly and for no apparent reason, one's subjects will be kept in a state of constant alert. A person who knows he has only to follow certain rules to stay safe ends up developing a sense of security that can pose a danger and push him toward rebellion. Whereas a subject kept in a perpetual state of uncertainty is prone to panic at any moment, and the idea of rebellion never enters his head. He's too busy fending off the light-ning bolts that might strike at any moment, without warning.

That was the kind of power Ksenia had over me. A panther, erratic and without mercy, she was at the same time completely defenseless. Her jealousy tor-mented her, and she was always ready to unmask you: You're not who you say you are, she'd say, you're petty minded, too, a traitor like everyone else. Curiously, though, things played out differently.

6

AS TIME WENT ON, Ksenia and I retreated into our own bubble. For us, the outside world only existed to accentuate our isolation. But just beyond, out there, lay a city brimming with possibility. Every day a former classmate would come by with an idea for some business opportunity. And while most of them were ridiculous, they still succeeded. Before you knew it, your classmate would move on from the shop where he had his shoes resoled to the custom Falcon he'd bought to take his family skiing in the Alps. One day, a friend would show up at a meeting on his grandfather's bicycle, the next in an armored Bentley with a phalanx of bodyguards.

That's more or less what happened to a guy I sometimes ran into when I'd leave the bubble I'd created around myself in order to meet with a few friends from high school, who'd recently repurposed themselves as businessmen. Mikhail had been the leader of the Young Communists at engineering school, but that's not to say he was a party apparatchik. In its final phase, the Komsomol attracted only the most cynical and ambitious guys, the ones who'd stop at nothing, the ones who wanted to make money. In the late 1980s, the only kind of company allowed in the Soviet Union was a students' cooperative, and these cooperatives became the business school for Russian capitalism. That's where most of our oligarchs got their education.

Mikhail belonged to this brash tribe. And though he tried several times to explain it to me, I never understood exactly what he was doing. He'd worked out a way to take a slice of the payments passing between state-owned companies. Basically, and I don't know quite how, he'd made himself a middleman who facilitated exchanges, borrowing money from some and lending it to others. It was a kind of small bank, several years before real banks were legalized.

It goes without saying that Mikhail's activities had little in common with those of a Swiss accountant. He took the capital he had access to and put it toward trafficking of every kind. He imported computers, manufactured souvenirs for tourists, opened factories for stonewashed jeans. He once told me that he'd come into a consignment of cognac bottles. At fifty dollars a bottle, he couldn't find a buyer. So he raised the unit price to five hundred dollars, and people fell over each other to take them off his hands.

Moscow was like that in those days. And Mikhail was in his element. He'd moved in a short time from wearing the shapeless jackets found in Soviet department stores to dark-purple Hugo Boss suits and then to custom-tailored clothing from Savile Row. His boyish, bespectacled face started appearing in the glossy magazines that chronicled Moscow's rapacious elite.

We would get together from time to time in the bar of the Radisson, the only luxury hotel in the capital at that time. I listened to his tales of adventure, vaguely thinking I might use them sometime for a play I wanted to write about people of his kind. One night, Ksenia came by to fetch me on our way somewhere. It was her first time meeting Mikhail. After the usual introductions, she stared at him for a moment: his little air of satisfaction, his piercing eyes behind the delicate titanium glasses, and his three-piece suit, in striking contrast with my slovenly sweatshirt.

"Where'd you get that awful tie?" she asked him point-blank.

I should have understood right then, from their first exchange, that my fate was sealed. That Ksenia was going to choose Mikhail, his vulgarity and his energy, his complicated watches and his English shoes. He knew straight off. He responded with a sarcastic smile and the name, I think, of a shop in Naples. I'll take you there once you're mine, his eyes said.

And I saw the whole thing. I saw it from the start. But for the longest time I refused to believe it. Ksenia was my goddess, capricious and vindictive. I lived in terror of her mood changes, and it never crossed my mind that a crocodile handbag and a suite at the Crillon were all that it took to win her favor. Each day, I laid at her feet the pearls I'd extracted from my painful delving in the realm of poetry, not realizing that a diamond bracelet would have had a more lasting effect. It's odd to notice just how hard our brain sometimes works to hide the truth from us. The clues are right in front of our eyes, but our minds refuse to assemble the pieces. After this first meeting, Mikhail started to visit our house regularly. He'd arrive alone or accompanied by one of a succession of young women chosen from the four corners of the empire for their luminous complexion and symmetric features. We would all pile into his Bentley, or his Jaguar, or his enormous Mercedes, and he would drive us to the best Georgian restaurant in town. Or he'd arrive at the door with two waiters, who would set out oysters and caviar on the table of our small suburban apartment. One day he even brought a sushi chef, flown in direct from Japan, who spent the evening slicing fatty tuna and yellowtail in the tiny workspace of our ten-square-foot kitchen.

Mikhail laid all these marvels at our feet with the slightly guilty air of a tradesman lighting a candle in church. And all along I thought it reflected a residual deference to the art Ksenia and I had sacrificed our lives to—as if culture in those years still exercised the slightest authority over the real world. I was wrong, of course, and Mikhail knew it. He pretended to admire our pathetic cultural relics, somewhat in the way you admire a child's drawings. I was blind, never noticing the condescension behind his gushing praise. Ksenia, as usual, noticed everything, and it pained her. She'd already started to suspect that culture was becoming a low-cost ornament, another gadget that the masters of the universe bought for themselves without a further thought. Mikhail's arrival, and his attitude, now confirmed this. It had irritated her at first. She'd caught on immediately to the existential threat that Mikhail posed—not just to us as a couple but to our whole world. The small, humble things we made, the carefully planned arabesques, all destined to be swept away by the dreams and aspirations of millions of faceless men and women on the currents of the new Russia. We were like maharajas reveling in the luxury of trained elephants and embroidered blouses, of cherry syrup and rose-petal sorbets, while ships carrying cargoes of race cars and private jets, of heli-skiing vacations and five-star hotels, were already on the horizon. With our American books and contacts in Berlin, we thought ourselves at the leading edge of the movement, when in fact we were the last ragtag stragglers still following a dead star, our parents'. We had thoroughly despised them for their cowardice, but they'd managed to pass on their passion for books and ideas, and for endless discussions about both. Mikhail was perfectly aware of all this. He was a native in the smooth, gleaming world of money, whose fiery power he knew, and nothing could have made him go back to before. But he wanted Ksenia, so he was willing to linger in our company, among the ruins of the city of the dead.

With the passing months, Ksenia became more receptive to his tributes. She didn't discuss it with me openly, but I sensed that she was growing increasingly nervous. My flaws, my lack of assertiveness, which she had initially attributed to a kind of old-fashioned Romanticism, she now felt as a chain constricting her growth and imprisoning her in a cramped world, just when she'd have liked to take full advantage of the possibilities of the new era. Mikhail showed up almost every day with new presents and new propositions. And though he tried to maintain the attitude of respectful humility he'd adopted when insinuating himself into our lives, I couldn't help noticing that his manner had grown more self-assured. The lectures, concerts, and late-night discussions that had marked the first phase of our relationship had all but disappeared, replaced by activities whose monetary heft was substantially greater, and where it was harder for me to maintain an acceptable standing. There were gallery openings, discotheque kickoffs, dinners at the White Sun or the Ermitazh, afternoon shopping expeditions, one event quickly following another, and I was starting to have a real problem with the stultifying boredom of all this flitting around.

Meanwhile Ksenia was becoming more and more intoxicated with Mikhail's lifestyle, to the point where it was hard for us to turn down even the most insignificant outings. All my attempts to slow the pace of our rendezvous met with sarcastic remarks and furious arguments. "Vadya has never liked going out," Ksenia would say with a disgusted grimace. "All he likes is to lounge around at home."

In truth, she was right. And sadly, Ksenia was neither pure enough nor corrupt enough to understand me.

I remember waking up one night and looking at her for a long time as she lay beside me, feeling that she had already moved on, a great distance away. To a place she'd return from only to deliver another contemptuous remark. I very much wanted her to come back. Look! It's me! Can't you see? But what had I to offer the vengeful goddess sprawled beside me, breathing quietly and regrouping her strength for the morning's combat? I went through life taking notes, as though preparing for an exam that never came. I felt exhausted, yet I still hadn't done anything. So many ideas flashed through my mind that taking any particular action seemed laughable. Every day my imagination suggested fifteen different lives to me, but nothing that I did in one ever proved useful in the next. So the only landing place that seemed worthy of my ambitions was the green velvet sofa in our apartment. At times, I managed to convince myself that Ksenia knew and saw my greatness. But day after day I could see that what at first had taken the form of irony was gradually turning into contempt.

It all brought me back to my childhood, to those autumn days in the country when the fog was so thick I couldn't see my hand in front of my face. "Go find the sun," my grandfather would say. So I'd go out into the woods and climb a hill overlooking the valley. And as I walked, the air would grow brighter and brighter until, miraculously, the sun would push through the layers of white haze and reveal a world where the frost-covered trees and bushes glistened with diamonds. I would gather a few branches covered in jewels to bring back to the house, but somehow the ice would melt on the way home, and I'd arrive holding nothing but a silly bouquet of brown branches. I don't have anything to prove, I told myself. But I was lying. I was running away. And Ksenia knew it. My longing for peace was perfectly sincere, but so far I'd done nothing to deserve it.

Suddenly Ksenia opened her ash-colored eyes, observing me. She showed not the least bit of surprise, as though it were perfectly normal to find me hunched over her as she slept, like a vulture at dawn. Nor did she show the least trace of friendliness. You're stronger than I am, I thought at the time, because you don't love me. To her, my suffering was just another annoyance.

One Saturday morning, we were in the country outside Moscow. Mikhail had organized an outing to an old dacha he was planning to buy. He'd brought along his latest trophy, I think her name was Marylène. She was French, worked for a big investment fund, and was cute, and she was also a good deal less flamboyant than the Circassian lovelies Mikhail generally had in tow. It looked to be a more serious relationship than usual. She, at any rate, seemed to think so.

The problem that day was that Marylène was not really used to the roads in provincial Russia. Or to Mikhail's Cossack style of driving. After a half hour of acrobatics on the dirt tracks near Vladimir, she felt sick. And despite his objections, she forced Mikhail to stop and turn the wheel of the Porsche over to me, threatening to hitchhike back to Moscow if he didn't. I tried talking her out of it, too, but couldn't, so I wound up sitting in the driver's seat with a comatose Marylène beside me, while Mikhail and Ksenia settled in the back seat behind us.

Not being used to driving a hundred-thousand-dollar car over sketchy gravel roads, I was a little nervous. And I was angry at myself for having landed again, for the umpteenth time, in a situation where I would show myself to disadvantage next to dashing Mikhail. He made fun of me: "OK, Vadya, show us what you can do. I'll bet within five minutes, Marylène is begging me to take the wheel again."

—Stop, Mikhail, said Ksenia, only seeming to defend me. Vadya drives perfectly well. You should see him on his grandfather's tractor.

—His grandfather's horse and buggy, you mean.

They were having a good time back there. Meanwhile, the Porsche moved along without much conviction in the direction I would indicate for it. Some aspect of the gearshift's workings never became quite clear to me, and I resolved the difficulty by staying in fourth. At a certain point I needed to adjust the rearview mirror. As I clumsily changed the angle, I saw into the back seat. Mikhail had his hand on Ksenia's knee. It sat there motionless, a giant snow crab.

It gave me a strange sensation. It's hard to explain, but I felt both a shock of surprise and the confirmation of something I'd already known. A satisfaction, almost. In any case, I let nothing show. I kept driving and carried on for the rest of the day as though nothing had happened. When we got back to the house, I told Ksenia I was leaving. She tried to make a scene, and if memory serves, she broke a glass or two. But deep down she was as relieved as I, though for different reasons.

7

I MOVED INTO A small room on the top floor of a low-income building made over by an architect friend into a kind of white capsule suspended above the turbulent swamp of Moscow. I'd expected a time of suffering. Instead, I once again felt light and strong. Apparently, I had less of a talent for love's sorrows than I'd thought. As someone said, no woman is more precious than the truth she reveals in making us suffer.

The theater, I now knew beyond doubt, could never satisfy the ambition that Ksenia's departure had awakened in me. I was now revolted by the mortal sadness of the man of letters, his inability to generate joy, his general unfitness for reality, the profound grief that trails him everywhere, his bereavement over the loss of culture, and his pathetic attempts to save its last shreds. Not to mention the "cultural life," made up of academia, prizes, and all the plotting on a minute scale by mediocre artists to maintain the illusion of survival, in the absence of any real talent.

I wanted to be a part of my times, not comment on them from the sidelines. And the farther I moved away from the library stacks, the more I became convinced that I could handle any opportunity that came my way. I just needed to find the moment on which to focus my whole life.

For the first time I allowed myself to drift on the dark current that was then coursing through the city. I met my neighbor Maksim, an advertising man who looked like Groucho Marx, always dressed in impeccable Italian suits and surrounded by spectacular women. "My ugliness sets me back about a week," he said, "ten days at most." He'd perfected the technique of showering his victims with a continuous stream of small attentions. Accustomed to more expedited courtships, they were taken completely by surprise. He could also be witty, especially about himself. Self-irony was another trait that was uncommon in our circles.

The upshot was that after a while, Maksim's prey not only gave in to his solicitations but also fell in love with him. Once the physical barrier was surmounted, they came to depend on his imagination, his intelligence, and his thoughtfulness. They also guessed that a strong character hid behind his gentle ways, a character more inaccessible than it might seem. By the end the roles would be reversed, and the women Maksim had courted now found themselves in pursuit, pressing their attentions on him and using every means to penetrate the secret of his mild indifference. Maksim did not capitalize on this, actually. When the roles did switch, he always remained generous to the female warriors who'd laid their arms at his feet. But it was also the signal he'd been expecting to set forth on a new conquest, which inevitably provoked a chain of more or less devastating explosions. I benefited from the constant maelstrom of women around him. Since my breakup with Ksenia, I'd needed a fresh outlook on life, and Moscow in the mid-1990s was the right place for that. You could leave the house in the afternoon to buy a pack of cigarettes, run into a friend who was for some reason in a state of high excitement, and wake up two days later in a chalet in Courchevel, half-naked, surrounded by slumbering young women, and have not the slightest idea how you had gotten there. Or you might go to a private party at a strip club, start talking with a stranger soaked to the gills in vodka, and find yourself the next day heading up a publicity campaign financed to the tune of several million rubles.

The unexpected has always been one of the great qualities of Russian life, but in that era it reached its climax. Imagine all these young men and women, bursting with life, many of them brilliant, geniuses even, who'd assumed they would be condemned to a dull, gray life and who suddenly found the whole world opening up to them. They could be anything they wanted, make money, travel the globe, sleep with

models. Things that only a few years before they hadn't
even dreamed existed. It was enough to make you lose
your head. And many did, literally. The level of violence was unimaginable—as if grammar school kids in
the city had been issued, along with their notebooks
and pencil sets, an arsenal of semiautomatic weapons. Gunshots rang out all over the place, over the
most trivial incidents. You'd see private militias, little
armies, forming an escort for perfect nonentities, and
you'd learn afterwards that one or another of them had
been obliterated. A bomb, or a hail of Kalashnikov bul-
lets. Everything contributed to feeding the radioactive
bubble that was Moscow. All the accumulated aspirations of the country, which had been immersed for decades in senescent Communist torpor, converged here.
And what was at the center wasn't culture, as the intellectuals believed, convinced that they'd inherited the
scepter when in fact they'd inherited nothing. At the
center was television. The throbbing heart of the new
world, which bends space-time with its magic weight
and projects the phosphorescent reflection of desire on
every side.

Leveraging my theater experience to enter a career
as a television producer was like going from a steam-
driven carriage to a Lamborghini. One day I was sitting
at a kitchen table expounding Mayakovski, drinking
scalding tea in a dense fug of unfiltered cigarettes,
and the next I was sipping cappuccinos in an open-
plan workspace conceived by Dutch architects, drafting

PowerPoint presentations and looking ahead to a vacation in Marrakech. In the studios of ORT, Russia's recently privatized Channel One, we were not just producing shows, we were experimenting with the forms of life that the mass of New Russians would soon be adopting. Our days, punctuated with "Oh my gods!" and "Whatevers," would wind up in a trendy wine bar with discussions on the relative merits of Sassicaia and Château Margaux. The women all took their cues from *Sex and the City*, and the men were Johnny Depp. We put the proverbial mimetic talent of Russians to use, acting out whatever could be considered *cool*, generating *buzz*, and spreading *hype*. The overall effect was patently ridiculous. Yet it was we who, during this phase, rebuilt the country's collective imagination. All the other institutions had crumbled, and it was up to television to lead the way. We took the rubble of the old system, the low-income housing of the suburbs, the towers of Stalinist skyscrapers, and made them into the offstage waiting rooms for our reality shows. Then we selected the most typical avatars of the Russian people—the drunken father, the babushka from the provinces, the calculating slut, the nihilist student—and we showed each of them the best way to enter and take part in the new world.

First rule: don't be boring. Everything else is secondary. The Soviets had tried to smother the country under an impenetrable blanket of boredom. Now anything was allowed, except monotony. Almost every day we came up with a new idea that was only slightly more preposterous than the last: A reality show about two outlaw gangs fighting for control of a small provincial town? Why not! A documentary on schools that teach young women how to ensnare top-earning men? Sounds good! Also, an astrologer who can predict the stock market? An interior decorator whose specialty is Marie Antoinette–style houses? Sign 'em up! Good to go!

We were creating a vulgar, barbaric TV, as the nature of the medium required. The Americans had nothing new to teach us, in fact we were the ones pushing the envelope when it came to trash broadcasts. Still, from time to time, the immortal Russian soul would rise from the depths. We had the idea at one point for a big patriotic show, and we asked our audience to tell us their heroes, the people who make Mother Russia truly proud. We were expecting the great minds: Tolstoy, Pushkin, Andrei Rublev, or possibly an actor or a pop star, as would happen in your country. But what did our viewers tell us, who did the formless mass of the people, accustomed to bowing their heads and looking at the ground, propose? Dictators! Their heroes, the country's founding figures, were all bloodstained autocrats: Ivan the Terrible, Peter the Great, Lenin, Stalin. We had to falsify the results to put Alexander Nevsky in first place—at least he was a warrior, not an exterminator. But the person with the most votes was Stalin. Stalin! Do you realize? It was at that point I understood that Russia would never be a country like the rest. Not that anyone ever thought otherwise.

8

AT THE TIME, ORT'S owner was a billionaire named Boris Berezovsky. He didn't seem, on first inspection, a particularly credible oligarch. Nothing about him suggested authority or inspired respect. He was short, pudgy, myopic, in constant agitation over some idea, or else busy laughing and making others laugh. Everyone knew how powerful he was, yet he felt a constant need to point it out. He loved being interrupted at meals by a phone call. "It's Tatiana," he would say with glowing eyes, "the president's daughter." Or else, "Ah! Anatoli," referring to the vice–prime minister. He couldn't take part in a conversation for more than four minutes without launching into a story about his astonishing exploits: how he'd once gone to Chechnya and arranged for all the hostages to be freed, putting up his ninety-thousand-dollar wristwatch as a pledge; or how, after taking over at Aeroflot, he'd designed the new uniforms for the stewardesses on a tablecloth in a restaurant.

He'd bought an old palace on Novokuznetskaya, a long, low, white building attached to the Church of Saint Clement. In theory, it should have been his company's headquarters, but Berezovsky had made it into something much more special, a kind of club. Logovaz House, as he called it, was open to business partners and generally to anyone he wanted to see, for whatever reason. You could drop in at all hours of the day and be sure to find a good cigar and a Belorussian entrepreneur or Kazakh general ready to remake the world with you. There was a gigantic aquarium that ran the length of the wall, a fireplace lifted whole from a Bavarian castle, and an inordinate accumulation of icons, ivory statuettes, and marquetry tables. From the tchotchkes to the rugs, the objects had clearly been chosen more for their monetary value than any aesthetic plan. Yet the whole had a certain charm, the upshot of an adventure that had ended well, a bank robbery, or a victorious night at the blackjack table. Uncle Vanya's house, redecorated by James Bond. Not the height of good taste, maybe, but most people who came there wanted just one thing: to stay as long as possible.

For a start, interesting people showed up at Logovaz House. Moscow's leading citizens, whether in politics, business, entertainment, or crime, all made appearances there. Then, at a certain hour, females of the species would start to filter in, as though arriving from another galaxy. What everyone wanted was the last possible appointment with Boris, because if you were still at the club at eight at night, you had an automatic invitation to one of Moscow's most enjoyable soirees. After that hour, work and pleasure melded entirely, and a meeting to discuss a business project could easily degenerate into an orgy. That's how power works in Moscow, it has never been divided from life. In your country, the men who hold power are just accountants. Gray figures who wake early in the morning, eat whole-grain muesli, and shut themselves in an office for ten, twelve, or fourteen hours to do what they have to do. Then they climb into their cars and ask to be driven home, or dropped off at a dinner party with other bores, or, at best, taken to see their mistress. End of story. In Russia, that would be inconceivable—we have a holistic conception of power.

In those days, my little successes as a television producer earned me an occasional invitation to Logovaz House. Berezovsky usually summoned me for news about a project in the audiovisual world, or because he had a cousin to recommend, or a ballet dancer. But one night, the conversation took an unexpected turn. We were sitting in his second-floor office with his longtime Georgian business partner. Both men complimented me on the ratings of my latest inanity and asked vaguely about my plans for upcoming programs, but I quickly sensed that something else was on their minds. At a certain point Berezovsky started to talk about politics.

He mentioned one of his minister friends, who had just been ousted from government. "Russian politics is Russian roulette," he said. "And the only question is whether or not you're ready to play."

Then Berezovsky turned toward me: "You see, Vadya, the beauty of Russia is that even when you don't gamble, you run all the same risks. Say you putter around quietly in your little corner, minding your own business. Sooner or later, a guy's going to show up who wants to strip you of everything you have. And if he's got a little power, or a little muscle, he may succeed. You're left there like a plucked goose, and what did you ever do to deserve it? So a person might as well play roulette, right?"

The tone Boris used always left you in some doubt. Was he just making a sociological comment, or did his words hide a somewhat less abstract element of threat?

"That's what happened to me," he said. "I was minding my own business off in my corner. I'd built up a classy little company, legitimate, modern, a Western-style operation with a network of dealerships selling lots and lots of cars in every part of the country. Then one day I discover there's some bastard who wants to take over my business. So what does he do? Does he set up a network of competing dealerships? Does he try to outperform me in the marketplace, the way you would in Europe or America? No! What the asshole does is load up an old Opel full of TNT and leave it parked along my route to work. So I drive by one afternoon, and BOOM! he hits the remote, no more Berezovsky. Or so he thinks. But it doesn't work, because Berezovsky has more lives than a cat. What happens is, I wind up holding my chauffeur's head in my lap—a piece of the fucking Opel sliced it off like a guillotine. As for me, not a scratch. Barely a bruise. People looked at my car, which had been carbonized, and they couldn't believe it."

Boris shook his own head, in a show of disbelief. "What can I tell you, Vadya? That day I realized that even if you don't pay any attention to power, power pays attention to you. I went to Switzerland for a two-week rest cure. And do you know what I did when I got back to Moscow? I joined the tennis club."

I knew the rest of the story. Everyone in Moscow knew it. At the time of the attack, the aged president Yeltsin was already on the decline. He rarely came into the office. He'd built himself a sports club on Sparrow Hills and spent all his time there, playing tennis. Or at home drinking. Around him, a small court of politicians and con men jockeyed for advantage. People who'd benefited enormously from their proximity to power but who were starting to worry that it might all vanish. The men were mediocrities with a special talent for stroking the vanity and exploiting the foibles of their leader. And Berezovsky struck them as a sort of messiah. His intelligence, his ambition, and his frenetic pace had quickly earned him the liking of the president's daughter, and through her, of the old bear himself. It has to be said that for them, Berezovsky seemed a godsend. He convinced them that all was not lost, that the president, battered though he was, could continue to hold power. "Little Father," I can almost hear him whisper into the old man's ear, "Russia still needs you, your courage, your integrity. You wouldn't want to leave the motherland to the Communists, would you?"

Riding this argument, Berezovsky managed to be put in charge of state television, which he then used to conduct an extraordinary reelection campaign. Within two months, the polls were showing that he'd made Yeltsin viable again, or rather he'd sunk all Yeltsin's rivals by suggesting that their election would bring back breadlines and Siberian gulags. The one slight problem was that the old man had another heart attack just two weeks before the election. That day, he was supposed to record a last appeal to the nation. The recording session was canceled, but rumors flew, and within days it was crystal clear that the president had to make an appearance. As Yeltsin was in no shape to go to the office, Boris gave orders that the furniture at the Kremlin was to be moved into the president's residence, so as to give the illusion that the president was fully functional. When the time came to record the message, Yeltsin was too weak to sit up in his chair, so they slipped a board behind his back to support him. That left just the speech itself, but the president was unable to articulate the words coherently. So he was asked to move his lips any way he could, and the entire broadcast was created in the editing room, using clips from his earlier speeches.

On Election Day, Yeltsin was in such poor shape he couldn't insert his ballot into the box. Berezovsky's cameras filmed him voting, then the two doctors in white coats supporting the president were edited out. The ridiculous maneuver worked, as they always do in Russia when there's enough resolve, and Yeltsin was reelected by a wide margin. Afterwards the old bear grew lethargic again, and Berezovsky became Russia's real boss.

Now that man was in front of me: "Russian politics is like Russian roulette, are you ready to risk it or not?"

Obviously I was up for the gamble. In a way, I'd never done anything till then but prepare for it.

"I don't know, Boris. I love my work."

—Right, and you're not so bad at it either. What I'm proposing is that you move to the next level. Berezovsky eyed me with all the intensity his thick lenses allowed. "What if you were to stop creating fictions and start creating reality?"

I had no idea what he was talking about. The Georgian sitting next to him smiled and nodded like a country cousin.

"You know I have a few contacts inside the Kremlin," said Berezovsky. Given the excessive modesty of his statement, I felt he expected a response, but I offered none; he continued, a little deflated. "In the past, I've been able to lend a hand from time to time, but at this stage the scenario has completely changed. It's not a question of supporting something that already exists, but of inventing something not yet in existence."

—As well as someone...the Georgian interjected.

—As well as someone, yes, of course, but the problem isn't there. What we need is to create a new reality. We aren't talking about winning an election, but about building a world.

Although Berezovsky spoke in general terms, I started to see what he was getting at. The next presidential election was barely a year away, and after two terms in office and five heart attacks, the old bear was out of the running. Berezovsky, however, had developed a taste for politics. And if the Communist threat was less pressing this time around, he still saw himself as the nation's savior. Or the puppet master who bends reality to his private interests. Which, in his mind, was all one.

"Our first priority is a political party," said Berezovsky. "I've already talked to Tatiana about it. We need to create the Unity Party. That's what's missing from the landscape. People have had enough of the Right, the Left, the Communists, the liberals—what they want is a sense of unity. The nostalgia they feel is not for Communism as such, but for order, the sense of community, the pride of belonging to something truly great. Russians aren't like Americans, and they never will be. It's not going to be enough for them to set aside a little money to buy a new TV. They want to be part of something that's like nothing else. They're ready to sacrifice themselves for that. Our duty is to give them back a perspective that looks beyond the next monthly car payment. Unity is what's needed. A movement that restores dignity to the people. I've already commissioned the graphic designers to come up with a logo. Here, Vadya, what do you think?"

Berezovsky handed me a drawing of a big brown bear in stylized profile. "Liberals have the fox, Communists the mammoth, and then there's the bear, symbol of the Russian soul—fierce, noble, powerful. That's what we need, Vadya. People have lost interest in politics, so we'll give them mythology instead!"

I remember Boris being so excited that he clumsily knocked over the penholder in front of him. Yet his thinking did make a certain amount of sense. In the early 1990s, Gorbachev and Yeltsin had led a revolution, but most Russians woke up the next day to a world that was unfamiliar, one they didn't know how to navigate. Before the American and the European dreams collapsed, there was the collapse of the Soviet dream. No one in your part of the world noticed, because it didn't seem possible that anyone could build a dream from such poor, colorless things: a respectable profession as a bureaucrat or a teacher, a compact Zhiguli, a dacha with a kitchen garden, vacations in

Sochi and occasionally in Varna, where you could wade in the Black Sea and look forward to a good barbecue with friends. Yet this model had a power and a dignity all its own. Its heroes were the soldier and the school-mistress, the long-haul trucker and the blue-collar worker—it was they who populated the billboards plastering the streets and subway stations. In a matter of months, all this was swept away. The new heroes, the financiers and the supermodels, took over, and the guiding principles of three hundred million inhabitants of the USSR were overthrown. They had grown up in a nation and now found themselves in a supermarket. The most shocking thing in this period was the discovery of money. Followed by the discovery that it might have no value at all, what with the stock market crash and inflation at 3,000 percent.

Berezovsky's intuition was dead right: the mood was changing. People were tired and wanted order again. They wanted things to make sense. The problem was to come up with an answer before someone else did.

9

BEREZOVSKY HAD ARRANGED TO meet me at the headquarters of the FSB, the KGB's successor. As he greeted me in the sepulchral lobby, he was all smiles, as if we were in the drawing room at Logovaz House. Perfectly at ease himself in this sinister place, he couldn't resist trying to scare me a little. "Do you know what Muscovites used to say about the Lubyanka building during Soviet times? That it was the tallest building in the city, because you could see Siberia from the basement."

It made me laugh, it was the kind of joke my grandfather would have told and my father not found funny. For my part, I was living on another planet. I thought we'd left that whole world behind, and I hadn't yet learned that nothing ever really goes away. Our visit, as far as I understood, was a matter of courtesy: it's always a good idea in Russia to maintain cordial

relations with the internal security apparatus. But while
we made our way down the long, windowless hallway
on the third floor, Boris told me otherwise: apparently,
our meeting was related to the conversation we'd had a
few nights before. "The head of the FSB would make a
good candidate. Nobody really knows him, but the old
man has confidence in the guy. He's proven himself at
decisive moments. He's young, competent, modern—
exactly what Russia needs. And he's modest, you'll see.
He didn't want to take over his predecessors' office, so
he turned it into a museum, a capsule from a time that's
gone forever."

True enough, after quickly passing through the re-
ception area, we were ushered into an office that could
have been the workplace of a department head in the
Postal Ministry. Its occupant was a pale blond man
with bleached features. He wore a beige polyester suit
and had the manner of an employee, leavened with
the barest hint of sarcasm. "Vladimir Putin," he said,
shaking my hand.

At the time, the tsar was not yet the tsar. His gestures did not then convey the inflexible authority they
would later come to acquire, and though his gaze had
some trace of the mineral quality we recognize in it
today, it was as if it were veiled by a conscious effort
to keep it under control. That said, his presence communicated a sense of calm.

Boris, in his trademark style, poured out a torrent
of words, all tending more or less in the same direction:

it was up to him, Putin, to take the reins of the situation and guide Russia into the new millennium.

The FSB director pushed back. "Listen, Boris, the secret service has all the advantages of politics without any of its drawbacks. I'm at the center of the system here, I see and hear everything that happens, and I'm well-positioned to protect the president and his family. I've done it before, and you know I'll continue doing it whenever necessary. If you transfer me into government, I'll be in the spotlight and unable to help anymore. And I'll end up ground down to a pulp, like all the other prime ministers these last few years. Right now you have a loyal guardian watching over your peace of mind, you don't want to lose that."

—I understand what you're saying, Volodya. But you have to keep one thing in mind: if we don't act quickly, a year from now there will be no president or presidential family to protect. And what do you think is the first thing the new boss in the Kremlin will do on entering office? He'll replace the FSB director, that's what he'll do.

Seated behind his rosewood desk, Putin appeared genuinely concerned. "That's possible," he said, "but there has to be another solution! Stepashin has been prime minister for only three months, why not stay with him?"

—It won't wash, Volodya. His favorability is at 3 percent. You know how public opinion works. It reaches a judgment quickly, and it's practically impossible to change it afterwards. People have seen Stepashin in action, and they don't think he's up to the task. The truth is, they're right. Can you picture Stepashin directing our army in the Caucasus? It would be like putting a Kalashnikov in the hands of a barnyard goose. Russia needs a real man, Volodya. A leader who will take them into the new millennium.

—I hear you, Boris, but what makes you think I am that leader? I'm a bureaucrat. All I've done my whole life is carry out orders and do my duty. I've spoken in public three or four times, and I can guarantee you the results were not brilliant. I've seen the president in action any number of times: he walks into a room, susses out the atmosphere, and a second and a half later he's got everyone eating out of his hand. He makes them laugh, he makes them cry, he builds a relationship with them as though he'd sat down with each of them at his kitchen table. Even today, even in his present state, he can still do it. People see him and they're moved. I'm not cut from that cloth.

—If I may, Vladimir Vladimirovich, that's exactly the point, I said.

Putin's frigid gaze came to rest on me for the first time. At my side, I sensed Berezovsky encouraging me to go on.

"The president has an uncommon personality, which it would be unreasonable to try to duplicate," I continued. "His human qualities were essential to our country's transition from the old Soviet Union to the

Russia of today. But after eight years in power, and given his physical condition, he cuts a fairly ragged figure. Polls tell us that the Russian people feel abandoned by him, that they like but don't admire him."

It was a delicate subject. But the head of the FSB offered no objections.

"That's why we think that a new person is needed, someone who would embody both an element of continuity and a clear break with the past. Were you to become prime minister, Vladimir Vladimirovich, you would automatically assume the mantle of legitimate authority. This is fundamental to Russians, who are not interested in adventure. What they want, especially right now, is stability and security. You'll also stand in marked contrast to the current president. You're young, athletic, energetic, and you strike one as able to shoulder all the responsibilities of leadership. Your history with the security services offers a guarantee of reliability. And your being a man of few words will stand you in good stead. The Russian people are fed up with smooth talkers. They want to be directed with a firm hand, they want someone who will bring order back to the streets and restore the state's moral authority.

"That's why we're envisioning a different kind of election campaign, one that's not about holding rallies or making election promises. In fact, just the opposite. The trick will be to present you as a politician who's not like all the rest.

"I don't particularly understand politics, Vladimir Vladimirovich, but one thing I do know is that it's a show. If I might ask you a question, do you know who's the greatest actress of all time?"

Putin shrugged impassively.

"Greta Garbo. And do you know why? Because an idol who withdraws from public view gains in power. Mystery creates energy. Distance fosters veneration. The imagination of Russian society, of any society, plays out in two dimensions. On the horizontal axis is proximity to everyday reality, while the vertical axis measures authority. In the past few years, Russian politics has occurred entirely along the horizontal axis, because that dimension was completely missing during the Soviet era. It made its appearance with Gorbachev, who would stop to talk to ordinary people—something no Soviet leader had ever dreamed of doing—and carried through to Yeltsin, who often seemed more a drinking buddy than a head of state.

"Today, though, the pendulum has clearly started swinging the other way. Too much horizontality has brought chaos, gunfire in the streets, state bankruptcy, and Russia's humiliation on the international stage. If you'll excuse the pun, the excess of horizontality has blotted out the horizon. What we need in order to establish perspective is elevation. All our data tells us that Russians today want verticality, which is to say authority. In psychoanalytic jargon, you could say the Russian people want a leader who'll leave off momspeak and go back to using the language of the father, to laying down the law. As the mayor of Moscow said when the government defaulted on its debt: 'The experiment is over.'"

—Except that he won't be the one to gain from it, said Boris, who had a series of ongoing issues with Moscow's first citizen.

—I believe Boris is right on this point, I said. Lujkov and ex–prime minister Primakov lead the polls because, unlike Yeltsin, they offer the prospect of a new beginning. But both have been around for a long time, and their image is almost as worn out as the president's.

The man beside me, one of the rare few to have a public image more shopworn than the politicians in question, nodded vigorously. I tried to ignore him and return to my point.

"You see, Russians have a very poor opinion of the governing class. And when politics gets a bad name, political experience becomes a handicap. That's why your lack of experience is an asset, Vladimir Vladimirovich. You're a fresh face, Russians don't know you and can't tie you to any of the recent scandals and mishandlings, which they blame on the people who've been in charge these past few years. Now, it's true as Boris said that the public forms its opinion quickly, so you'll only have a few months to convince the Russian people that you're the man for the job. But we firmly believe you have the requisite qualities."

—That's right, Volodya, we're certain of it, said Berezovsky. And don't forget that you won't be alone.

I'll be beside you every step of the way, ready to help and give advice whenever you need it.

I could be wrong, but I seemed to detect in Putin, who'd stayed motionless since the beginning of the conversation, the tiniest glimmer of irony in reaction to these words. Whatever the case, Boris made his way back to the club in high spirits.

"It's a sure bet," he kept saying to anyone who'd listen, "we've found our winning horse. Not that he's any kind of Nobel prizewinner, but he'll do just fine for the task at hand. He has the right build for the part. We just need to put him into the hands of our little communications wizards, and they'll turn him into Alexander Nevsky. Or Greta Garbo. Right, Vadya?"

And he laughed with childish glee.

The fact that I'd told the former head of the KGB to model himself on an old-time American actress struck him as hilarious. I shrugged and laughed along with him, but the truth is that this first meeting with the tsar had left an odd taste in my mouth. I couldn't exactly pinpoint it, but I felt that things were a little more complicated than Berezovsky was making them out to be.

Throughout the meeting, Putin had behaved with impeccable courtesy toward Boris. Deference even, as he listened to the businessman's advice. Yet when Berezovsky addressed him in his usual familiar way, I thought I saw a trace of irritation in Putin's eyes. And then there'd been that glimmer of irony at the end, when Boris promised to guide him step-by-step. As if the FSB chief found the mere thought of taking this man's guidance highly comical.

Berezovsky clearly hadn't noticed any of this, but it wasn't long before my suspicions were confirmed. I was in the editing room a few days later when my telephone buzzed insistently. "Vadim Alexeievich?" said a voice, "this is Igor Sechin, secretary to Vladimir Putin. The director would like to invite you to join him for lunch next Tuesday." Although the invitation was couched in polite terms, the voice on the other end of the line entertained no possibility of a refusal on my part. A male secretary, I noticed in passing—a sign of distinction among the old Soviet guard. A fact that I, unlike Berezovsky, was ready to pick up on.

10

OUR LUNCH TOOK PLACE at a French restaurant that had recently opened on a street off the Arbat. I was a little surprised at the choice, having formed a fairly austere image of Putin at our first meeting. Sechin, the secretary, was standing by the door when I arrived. "Hurry, Vadim Alexeievich," said Sechin, "Vladimir Vladimirovich is already here!" The idea that a nonentity like me could leave his boss waiting clearly irritated him.

Once inside, I found Putin sitting alone at a large corner table, set back somewhat from the others. His expression was relaxed, his gestures calm. He radiated an impression of cold power that he'd clearly chosen not to display at our earlier meeting.

He shook my hand, still seated, then turned toward the maître d'hôtel, who was eyeing him with the hypnotized attention of a small rodent looking at a rattlesnake: "Give us your advice, Pavel Ivanovich."

—If you're thinking of fish, I'd recommend the scallops with a cauliflower mousse or the sole cardinale with flambéed shrimp. If you'd prefer a meat dish...

—A bowl of kasha, please.

—Two.

The maître d' suppressed a shudder and marched off. It was the first time I would notice Putin's complete indifference to food, just as I would later witness his imperviousness to the other pleasures that make life agreeable. As Faust says, "He who would command must find his happiness in commanding."

Meanwhile, the FSB chief had already turned to the matter at hand: "I have great respect for Berezovsky and I'm grateful to him for his offer. An undertaking of the kind we're considering requires enormous effort, and Boris has already shown that he can perform miracles. At the same time, I'm not a sixty-eight-year-old man who has come through five heart attacks. If I decide to commit to this plan, I'll be relying on my own strength, not someone else's. I'm used to executing orders, and in a sense I find it the most comfortable position for a man to be in. But Russia's president can't be taking orders from anyone. The idea that his decisions might be influenced by private interests is absolute anathema to me."

Putin's gaze, on that day, was considerably more penetrating than it had been during our meeting with

Berezovsky. He looked deep into my eyes to gauge the effect his words were having.

"Given the way you were brought up, Vadim Alexeievich, I think you can understand what I'm talking about."

This was certainly true. The idea that the state had a certain moral superiority over the private sector was deeply ingrained in me. The sight of Boris and his gang ripping at top speed down Moscow's reserved lanes, sirens blaring, deeply offended me, just as it offended most Muscovites.

"I was struck by your analysis the other day," said Putin. "I've looked into your background, and I think you could make an important contribution to the work I do, whatever that turns out to be, either now or later. But we need to be clear on one point. For all that I respect Berezovsky, I'm not about to put myself in his hands. If you accept my offer, Vadim Alexeievich, you'll work exclusively for me. The administration will guarantee you a salary, though it will be less, I'm afraid, than what you're earning now, and you'll have to make do with it. I won't tolerate any bonus, any benefit coming to you from Boris or anyone else. If it's money that interests you, keep your job in the private sector. When you work for the state, you have to put the public interest above everything else, even your own interests. And if you do agree to work for me, I don't have to tell you that I have ways of making sure that you respect our bargain."

He didn't exactly waste any time. I'd grown accustomed, during my brief career as a television producer, to being courted, and it would have given me
pleasure to take the FSB chief's curt offer, crumple it
up, and toss it on the floor. The problem was that he'd
analyzed the situation correctly. He'd understood that
money meant less to me than other things, and certainly less than the chance to take part in the kind of
undertaking Putin seemed to have in mind. No point
beating around the bush when you can go straight to it.
I would later see that the tsar always operated this way.
He'd arrive at the crux of an issue before anyone else
and then go for it bluntly. Fuck the niceties.

"I've thought about your concept of verticality,"
Putin continued. "It's interesting, but it can't hang in
the air like a red balloon. It has to be buttressed on
the ground and applied to an actual circumstance. The
country is in chaos and requires a steady hand, but it
would be delusional to think that you could solve all the
country's problems at once. We need a clearly defined
situation where we could restore vertical power immediately and specifically. Otherwise we'd run the risk of
getting off track and looking as ineffective as the rest."

—True, Vladimir Vladimirovich, but things always
happen, the unexpected crops up.

—Trust me, Vadim Alexeievich, the unexpected is
always the result of incompetence. Besides, wasn't it
your old friend Stanislavski who said that technique is
not enough, that true creation calls for the unexpected?

The same trace of irony that I thought I'd seen at the Lubyanka glinted in Putin's eyes again, although this time more openly. For my part, I was floored. I'd have sworn that as recently as last week he'd hardly heard of Stanislavski.

"The perfect setting is right in front of us," said Putin. "The country is under pressure. The Islamic fundamentalists are looking beyond Chechnya. They're now setting their sights on Dagestan, Ingushetia, and Bashkiria, and from there they'll move into the heart of the country. If we don't stop them, in a few years there will be nothing left of the Russian Federation."

—Excuse me, Vladimir Vladimirovich, but that's one hot mess I'd think twice before wading into. In just the last few years, Chechnya has killed more political careers here in Moscow than combatants on the battlefield.

—Because none of the politicians addressed the situation forcefully enough. They wanted to make war without declaring it, conduct a humane, American-style conflict, and you can see where that got them. The Islamists massacred them. What I'm talking about is different. I have no interest in winning the Nobel Peace Prize. What does interest me is wiping out the separatists and the threat they pose to the integrity of the Russian Federation.

—I won't argue the geopolitics, Vladimir Vladimirovich, because I know nothing about it. But what I can say is that this would be political suicide.

—That's where you're wrong, Vadim Alexeievich. You've swallowed the Western notion that an election campaign consists of two teams of economists debating over a PowerPoint document. It doesn't work that way. In Russia, power is something else entirely.

I wasn't sure at the time exactly what Putin was getting at. But I went away from our lunch certain of one thing: Berezovsky had made a big mistake. The man I had just eaten with would allow no one in the world to tell him what to do. You could accompany him, maybe, and I intended to try to, but you certainly couldn't lead him. And Boris needed to wake up to that as soon as possible.

I I

WHOEVER LIVES IN THE Kremlin owns time. All around the fortress things are in constant flux, while on the inside life seems to have stopped, marked only by the solemn strokes of the Spasskaya Tower clock and the regular rounds of the presidential guard. As has been the case for centuries, a person crossing the threshold of the gigantic fossil that Ivan the Terrible placed in the center of Moscow feels the hand of limitless power resting on him, a power accustomed to grinding men's fates to dust with the ease of caressing a newborn's head. This force spreads outward in concentric circles through the city streets, giving Moscow that looming sense of menace that is a large part of its charm. The unsightly bulk of the Lubyanka, along with the seven towers that ring the central avenues, the skyscrapers of modern-day Moscow-City, and the rococo villas of

Rublyovka are reflections of the dark energy flowing from the fortress's heart.

But in the summer of 1999, that spell was broken. All that emanated from the great rooms of the presidential palace was the alcoholic breath of a fat and tired Siberian bear, surrounded by a small retinue of bejeweled courtiers who were growing increasingly alarmed at seeing the man to whom they owed their fortunes fall apart. Yeltsin had become a deadweight. Not only could he no longer protect them, but he was likely to drag them all into the abyss.

Outside, the animal city could feel that the jaws of authority had loosened their grip. Moscow was no longer the empire's capital. It had become a metropolis where cell phones rang during performances of the Bolshoi Ballet and gangsters settled their scores with automatic rifles, enforcing the law of the jungle. The Kremlin no longer set the tone—money did that now. And the armored Mercedes of the oligarchs bulled through the streets of the city center just as in tsarist times the coachmen of the nobles had cleared a path through the crowds, cracking their whips to left and right. Meanwhile, when the docile working class of Moscow arrived home from work, they didn't even have the money to turn on the heater.

In early August, the old bear picked a new prime minister whom most people had never heard of. Vladimir Putin's nomination met with general skepticism.

This was the fifth head of government Yeltsin had named in just over a year. "There's no point ratifying the appointment," the leader of the Duma had said. "There'll be someone new to take his place in two months anyway." Putin saw it differently. He knew he had only a few weeks to make his mark on public opinion, and he didn't plan to waste any time.

Our offices were not in the Kremlin but in the old House of Soviets, also known as the White House—a gigantic block of naphthalene set down on the banks of the Moskva River, which nonetheless failed to protect the country from moths. Originally intended to host gatherings of the Supreme Soviet, the building now housed, more modestly, the government of the Russian Federation. After the old bear shelled the upper floors with mortar rounds during a moment of irritation, a Swiss firm had come in to rebuild, but the place hardly gave a sense of Alpine efficiency. The hallways were full of reassuring-looking types, old-fashioned characters in dark-gray and brown clothes. They seemed to exist outside the present moment, sculpted in wax, holdovers from a world where time was measured in great slabs, in contrast to the frenetic pace of the city, the frantic whirl of dollars and cameras I'd been a part of.

On the prime minister's designated floor, twenty or so rooms had been emptied for the incoming staff. We moved in there: Putin, his administrators, the economic and military advisors, and the communications personnel. We worked day and night. The antiseptic walls could barely contain the violence of our ambitions. Meanwhile, only meters away, career government employees went about their lives, as placid as a lullaby sung by a nineteenth-century babushka. I'd subsequently learn that it's always this way in a ministry. A small group of people works frenetically in one room, and everyone else slacks off. Interaction between the two groups is limited—an occasional respectful glance, tinged with irony, as the longtimers wait for this umpteenth invasion to move through like the rest, in the full knowledge that the grass will grow again where it's now being trampled.

I don't think they'd understood that we were it, that our gang was there to stay. How could they? We looked like everyone else. In our custom-tailored suits, carrying laptops, wearing the haughty expressions of people who have all the answers because they're fluent in English. I struck them as being different, though. Sometimes one of these ministerial wraiths would stop me in the hallway. "Might I trouble you for a moment, Vadim Alexeievich?"

—Of course, I'm all ears.

—I just wanted to say I knew your father. A great man. Those were the days... They don't make men of his stamp anymore!

Some undoubtedly said this to flatter me. More often, though, the specters who briefly interrupted me just wanted to make contact. Finding someone in our

faction who'd known the old world reassured them.
And do you know what? It reassured me too. Each time
one of those people, seemingly escaped from the pages
of a Gogol novel, spoke my father's name, I felt a surge
of warmth, and my childhood years came back to me,
the fur coats and official cars, the piroshki and cutlets
of Granovskovo Street. I would see the same nostalgia
in their eyes. They remembered me as a child, or at
least another like me, maybe their own son. They'd
had plenty to be proud of at the time. They worked for
the Supreme Soviet, for the Central Committee. They
would arrive home and tell their children: "Today, I
saw Comrade Gromyko, he was just back from Kabul,
looking pleased about something. Things are clearly
going better over there in Afghanistan."

In fact, it was all over, and it had been for some
time. But they still believed in the old order, or they
could at least pretend to believe in it without anyone
telling them they were misguided. Now they'd lost the
right even to pretend. They could still take pride in their
many years of service, however, their ability to look at
new arrivals through a long lens. In their presence, I felt
closer to my father, I understood for the first time what
had happened to him. With some surprise, I discovered
that I, too, had the gene that allows you to adapt to this
kind of life—to live the way you might read through a
stack of newspapers, wanting to be done with it.

True, I worked eighteen hours a day. Sitting beside
the prime minister, I took part in a constant stream of

meetings, and historic decisions were taken at every one of them. But the more deeply I entered into the process of governing, the more full of misunderstanding the world seemed, the more choked with useless explanations and missed opportunities. A vast exercise, never-ending, that consumed whole lives without leaving a trace. How could I have thought to leave a mark on the surface of the mute and indifferent sea?

It was at this point that the unexpected happened. On an autumn night a little after midnight, when the good people of Moscow had retired under the covers, leaving the city to the mobsters and the supermodels, a tremendous rumble echoed through the darkened capital. On Guryanova Street on the outskirts of Moscow, several hundred kilos of explosives had blown a nine-story apartment building apart. Dozens of peacefully sleeping families were swallowed up in the explosion. Four days later, a second explosion occurred at five in the morning. Another suburban building had been destroyed, leaving more than a hundred dead.

Afterwards, there were people who said the bombs had been set off by Putin's allies, by agents of the security services. Frankly, I don't know what's true. If it's a secret that has remained closely guarded, I'm glad to say no one has ever shared it with me. That said, it's my experience that things are generally simpler than they appear. In politics, a cure is worth any amount of prevention. If you stop an attack from taking place, nobody is going to know, while if you react to one decisively and nail the guilty parties, then yes, you'll derive political capital from it. But it's a long way from that to saying that the bombs were set off by the FSB and not by Chechen terrorists.

In any event, those bombs were our 9/11 moment, two years early, and they completely transformed the landscape. Up to that point, the war in Chechnya had been a distant engagement that mattered only to the families whose sons were serving in the military over there. They formed a tiny minority. But when buildings in the suburbs of Moscow started to blow up in the middle of the night, carrying off hundreds of solid Russian citizens while they slept, the war came home to Russians for the first time.

Our people are valiant, and they are used to making sacrifices. But after those bombs exploded, there was a panic such as I'd never seen before. People were afraid to go home and sleep. They organized night watches around their houses, and if anyone wandered into the neighborhood who had even a trace of a beard, there was a good chance he'd be beaten to death.

Fortunately, the state was in the hands of a leader who was capable of responding. People tend, looking back, to attribute supernatural powers to the tsar, but the truth is that the only indispensable quality for a man of power is the ability to make use of circumstances. Not pretend to control them, but make decisive use of them.

Putin has never been fond of public speaking, but it was clear that the people needed to hear his voice. We were in Kazakhstan on a state visit. Just as well, because the Kremlin's gilded panels would have distracted from the message. We needed a simpler location, the rough look of an improvised council of war. The press conference started with a few technical questions about the time it took emergency services to show up, the status of the investigation. The prime minister answered with his characteristic calm, precisely and without a trace of emotion—very much the ascetic government official that Russians were starting to recognize. Then a journalist asked him a slightly more polemical question: "Apparently, you responded to the attacks by ordering a bombing raid on the Grozny airport. You don't think this kind of action might just aggravate the situation?"

What happened then is something I'm still not able to fully explain. Putin stayed silent for a moment. And when he resumed speaking, his expression hadn't changed, but his presence had taken on a different consistency, as if his body had been dipped in liquid nitrogen. The ascetic official had suddenly transformed into the angel of death. It was the first time I'd seen a phenomenon of this kind. Never, even on the stages of the best theaters, had I witnessed a similar transfiguration.

"I'm tired of answering questions like this," he snapped, not even looking at the journalist who'd asked it. "We'll hit the terrorists wherever they're hiding. If they're in an airport, we'll hit the airport, and if they go take a shit, pardon my language, we'll get them in their outhouses."

At this remove, it might not sound like much or might just strike you as vulgar, but you have no idea the impact these words had on the public. It was the voice of command and control. Russians hadn't heard it in a long time, but they recognized it immediately, because it was the voice their fathers and grandfathers had grown up with. A great sigh of relief swept over Moscow's avenues and fearful suburbs, over Siberia's endless forests and plains. There was again someone at the top who could guarantee order.

That day, Putin stepped fully into his role of tsar. As for me, it reminded me of one of my grandfather's sermons. "Do you know what the problem is?" he asked one day when we were walking through the woods near his *isba*. "The human eye was made to survive in the forest. That's why it's sensitive to movement. Whenever something moves, even on the extreme edge of our field of vision, our eye captures it and sends the information to our brain. But do you know what we don't see?" I shook my head. "What stays motionless, Vadya. In the middle of all the changes, what we're not trained to perceive are the things that stay the same. And it's a big problem, because when you think about it, the things that don't change are always the most important."

It's a lesson I've never forgotten. None of us has. It's why, when the tsar talks politics, he never mentions numbers. His language speaks of life, of death, of honor, of country. Governing is not an activity that can be left to the feckless, to those who are too lazy to make money, too timid to become rock stars. Accountants looking for glory, little men who think that politics boils down to running a building council.

That's not what it is at all. Politics has just one goal: to address men's terrors. Consequently, when the state no longer manages to protect its citizens from fear, the very basis of its existence is called into question. When the battle over the Caucasus moved to Moscow in the fall of 1999 and nine-story buildings started to fritter away like sandcastles, the good Muscovite, already somewhat disoriented, saw the specter of civil war rising before him for the first time. Anarchy, dissolution, death. Primordial terror, which even the dismantling of the Soviet Union had failed to awaken, started seeping into people's minds. What's going to happen to me?

Vertical power offers the only satisfactory answer, the only one that can appease man's anxiety when exposed to the world's ferocity. After the bombs went off, reestablishing the vertical of power became the tsar's top priority. Moving on from the Western logic of commodities and gadgets, of debates between bureaucrats mesmerized by statistical graphs, to build instead a system that would answer to man's fundamental needs. That was the mission we then embarked on. Deep politics, night and day, uninterruptedly.

12

ON THE MORNING OF December 31, 1999, a day when your newspapers were full of ridiculous articles about the Y2K bug, the software glitch that would supposedly make computers go haywire and planes drop from the sky, Putin called me into his office. "Tell me, Vadim, did they teach you to skydive at the Academy of Theater Arts?"

The question struck me as uncalled for, and I said nothing.

"But they'd at least have taught you how to pretend, no?"

A familiar gleam sparkled ironically in the tsar's eyes. Standing next to him, Sechin was enjoying the scene with all the relish of a Doberman that has finally gotten to eat the cat in the neighbor's yard. As I still said nothing, Putin added curtly: "In any case, get ready. We leave this afternoon."

As announced, we made our way to the military airport a few hours later, where a plane was waiting to take us to the capital of Dagestan. From there we loaded onto three helicopters, heading for Gudermes, in Chechnya. We immediately started to breathe in the air of excitement and madness that surrounds a war, when just staying alive is itself an adrenaline rush. It was all new to me. My last remnants of inherited privilege had allowed me to avoid military service at eighteen. Now, while I listened distractedly to Putin's exchange of pleasantries with the officers and had my first whiff of the fumes of war, I started to understand why some men might prefer them to any other stimulant. Unlike the civilian helicopters I'd ridden until then, this one had no opening to the world outside. We were inside an armored cabin, suspended over the Caucasus in the dark of night, and that simple fact turned us within minutes from being strangers to brothers, united not so much by fear as by the imperative not to let the least trace of fear show. Despite the deafening noise of the helicopter's blades, we all felt the need to make conversation. We started by trading New Year's memories from our childhoods. Some had grown up in tiny villages, in Kazan or Novosibirsk, but none of us, as we quickly realized, had ever imagined spending New Year's Eve in a helicopter with the tsar. Putin, sitting in the front row, constantly turned back to us, and we could see from his expression that his wonder and amazement were even greater than ours. Against all odds, he was now tsar.

At a certain point, someone realized that it was
almost the stroke of midnight. Sechin, who hadn't yet
developed his acquaintance with the French *grands crus*,
produced a bottle of Moldavian champagne. We toasted
to the health of the Russian people, and to the troops
that we were going to visit, but just then the pilot informed us that he would be unable to land. He needed
visibility of one hundred and fifty meters, and he had
only a hundred meters, or something of the kind. The
atmosphere changed immediately. The tsar insisted that
we had to land, but when he understood that it wasn't
going to happen, he walled himself in silence. The
helicopters turned around. Everyone thought the mission had been aborted. Actually, someone remarked
in chiseled tones, there were plenty of troops for us to
review in Dagestan. We could always go to Gudermes
another day.

I made a point of saying nothing at all. Advising
a ruler to abdicate is never a good idea, even in the
most trivial matters. In fact, the helicopters had barely
landed back where they'd started when we realized
that, if Chechnya was where the tsar wanted to celebrate New Year's, then Chechnya was where we'd
be going, even at the risk of setting off a landmine or
plunging into a crevasse. At one o'clock in the morning, we loaded onto jeeps and headed for the pass in
the mountains. For an eternity, immersed in total darkness, we drove along the Caucasus's ravines. Unable to
see, we sensed in the shadows around us a cold, black,

wind-battered landscape and the indomitable will of the man who led us. It took nearly four hours, but we arrived in Gudermes a little before dawn. The soldiers were sleepy and surprised. They couldn't believe the tsar had taken so much trouble to visit them. Most were just kids in military fatigues, rubbing their eyes as though it might be a fairy tale.

After briefly passing the troops in review, we found ourselves in a tent with thirty or so officers. There, you could feel the situation stripped to its bare essentials, as in the Iron Age. The visit from the government authorities was impressive, no doubt, but we were in a place where authority was earned on the battlefield. The nearness of death simplified things a great deal. Polite formulas had no place here. The men looked at Putin with that mix of deference and irony that characterizes Russian attitudes toward power. They seemed to be waiting for something. A photographer who'd traveled with us took pictures of the event. It was hard not to act the part of tourists. To celebrate the New Year, the unit commander had set out champagne for a toast. All eyes turned to the tsar. But Putin, a glass of champagne already in hand, paused the proceedings.

"Let's stop for a moment," he said, his hard gaze traveling over the assembled men, "I would like to drink to the health of the wounded and extend New Year wishes to everyone here. But we face many obstacles on the road ahead. Many hard tasks confront us. You know this. And you know what the enemy has planned for you. We know it too. We know the strikes they are preparing, and where they will occur. We can't allow ourselves an instant of weakness. Not one second. If we lower our guard, the dead will have died in vain. So I propose to you that we put our glasses back on the table. We will drink together, but at a later time."

I hadn't suggested it to him. I don't think he'd planned his gesture beforehand. But it affected everyone present as if he'd dumped a bucket of ice water over their heads. In that instant, the tsar and the members of the military became one and the same, like a family in the midst of a conflagration, bound together by love and pride. After that, surrounded by officers, the tsar handed out medals and hunting knives to the soldiers: "You're not here just to fight for our country's honor and dignity," he told them, "you're here to put a stop to the disintegration of Russia."

That night on the news, Russians saw their soldiers, tears welling in their eyes, showing a pride and determination not seen in years. Because once again they had a leader in charge.

That's when I started to suspect that Putin belonged to what Stanislavski called the tribe of great actors. He believed that actors come in three kinds. The first has instinctive talent, and when he's on his game he can transport an audience. But it's different on his off days, when he becomes overemphatic and embarrassing. That's the kind of actor who can ruin a production all on his own. Then there's the methodical actor, the one who studies the part, does breathing exercises, devotes his evenings to rehearsing gestures and intonations. That one, by contrast, won't lead you to great heights of emotion, but he also won't disappoint you. He always does what needs doing, and you can count on his unvarying clichés in every circumstance. Putin is neither of these. Like all great politicians, he belongs to the third kind: the actor who puts his own self on stage, who doesn't need to act because the role is so thoroughly a part of him that the plotline of the play has become his own story, it flows in his veins. When a director finds himself with a talent of this magnitude, he has practically nothing to do. He just needs to follow. Avoid introducing complications. Give his actor a little nudge from time to time. That's how the election campaign went. In theory, I was its director, its strategist, to use a term of Boris's, who thought *he* was the strategist. None of that was the case. Putin was already manning the controls. Alone.

While this was all happening, Berezovsky was still living in a dream world. He badgered the tsar with phone calls and meeting requests. He put himself forward as a mediator to deal with Chechnya, as an ambassador to Europe, as the Moscow campaign director. There's nothing worse than the virus of politics. Especially when it infects someone without the antibodies

to combat it. Boris was a very intelligent man. But intelligence doesn't protect you from anything, not even
stupidity.

I remember a meeting in the tsar's office at the
White House. Berezovsky hadn't seen Putin in several
weeks and was even more agitated than usual. "We're
becoming too negative, Volodya, too dark. There's
nothing wrong with war, and we all know that you're
a great general, that you'll lead us to victory—I'll even
build you a triumphal arch if you like. But do you
know what Julius Caesar did when he returned from
Gaul? He went into debt up to his ears to give the
Romans a three-week celebration. *Panem et circenses*,
Volodya, does that mean anything to you? In your case,
you don't even have to go into debt, because I'll pay for
it. But let's give these poor Russians something, otherwise they won't go to the polls, they'll be too busy
jumping out of windows!"

In fact the person who wanted to jump out the
window was Berezovsky himself, and the tsar knew
it. Boris needed to feel indispensable, but he sensed
that his usefulness was diminishing by the day. The
noncampaign that I'd set up for Putin hadn't cost a
ruble, whereas Boris needed to build up credit with
his candidate. He wanted us to use him, use his television stations, use his dark money to pay for television ads, posters, rallies. "They tell me you've even
turned down the free advertising slots on TV? At that
rate people will forget you're a candidate, Volodya.

They'll think you're bowing out in favor of Luzhkov or Primakov."

"Don't be absurd, Boris." It was the first time I'd heard the tsar speak so sharply to Berezovsky. "We're the government. The news is our campaign, the actions we're taking, the history we're writing. No one believes advertisements anymore. Facts are the only advertising that interests us."

Berezovsky was jolted as if a scorpion had bitten him. For a tiny moment I thought he'd finally realized the depths of his misjudgment. But of course I was wrong. Boris had advanced too far down his own road. Years of making bets that had paid off handsomely and enjoying unlimited power had fattened him like a Christmas turkey. He'd lost his ability to gauge power relations accurately. Instead of analyzing the real dynamics of what was happening in front of him, he'd grown used to evaluating everything in terms of personal relationships. True, he had helped the tsar rise to power. And I might add that Putin is no ingrate. He doesn't repay the people who've helped him by sending them to work in the salt mines. There, at least, Berezovsky had been right. The tsar genuinely felt gratitude and acted accordingly.

But he was a man destined for power. He was drawn to it, understood it, needed it. I don't know how Boris could have imagined that after climbing to the throne, the tsar would agree to share the scepter with him. Or even consider letting one of his subjects stand on equal footing. You only had to look at him for a moment to realize this. But that was the problem: Berezovsky had never spent a moment looking carefully at Putin. He'd seen him as a silent enforcer and never once imagined that Putin's impassive reserve hid anything but a plodding and obliging nature.

While all of us do some things better than others, I've rarely seen a person combine such keen intelligence with such abysmal stupidity as Berezovsky. He could engineer the most complicated deals and make a vast treasure appear out of nowhere, like a genie out of a bottle. But he completely missed things that would have been obvious to his lowest underling. In the final analysis, I think he was so intent on himself that he never had time to observe others, a failing that would cost him in the end.

13

THE TSAR HAD RESTORED the vertical of power, and the voters rewarded him for it. We won the elections in the first round, without a runoff. But the battle against the forces threatening to tear the country apart had only just begun, the most dangerous enemies being in our own camp. After Putin's election, Berezovsky sat and waited. He stopped assaulting the Kremlin with phone calls. And although one of his reporters criticized the inauguration for its excess of pomp, and others made ironic comments about new government appointees, it was clear that Boris was waiting for something else: the chance to make the tsar realize who was really in charge. And one day, the opportunity arrived.

It was mid-August, and Putin had left Moscow to vacation in Sochi. In those days, the tsar wasn't particular about his distractions. He hadn't yet met Berlusconi,

wasn't yet into limited-edition Patek Philippe watches
or three-hundred-sixty-foot yachts. A few days of
state-supplied luxury in the CPSU secretary's former
summer residence with his wife and daughters, a boat
outing, and a barbecue of pork and sturgeon in sunny
weather amply satisfied the simple tastes of the functionary he had only just stopped being.

But no more than a few days into his sojourn in
Sochi, the tsar's rest was abruptly interrupted when a
nuclear submarine belonging to the Russian navy sank
in the Barents Sea. There were about a hundred crew
members on board, some of whom died immediately,
while the remainder were trapped on the seafloor. At
first, we tried to keep the incident a secret, following
our usual custom, but within two days the news had
started to leak, we weren't sure how.

Berezovsky pounced like a bear stalking its prey
on the river's edge. His television station, ORT, interrupted programming to provide live, continuous coverage of the event. They rented a helicopter to fly over
the sector where the sub had gone down. They traveled
to European capitals to interview experts, who asked
why the Russian authorities were refusing Western offers of help in rescuing the sailors. They aired segments
in which engineers analyzed the probability of asphyxiation and psychologists gave minute descriptions of
claustrophobia. And then there were the families. Reporters went and found the relatives of the trapped sailors, one by one. Every babushka had a lacerating tale

to tell, every fiancée had a portrait of the hero who'd sunk to the seafloor while defending his country. All of them were angry at the government, which had at first acted as though nothing were happening and then failed to mount even a rudimentary rescue operation.

They're choking for air down there! Our boys are dying of asphyxiation! A chorus of anguish went up from the innards of the Russian people. Or at least that's how Berezovsky's television station painted it. And where was the tsar while all this was happening? By the Black Sea, taking his vacation! Riding his water skis! A monster. Incompetent. The talking heads didn't hold back. For the first time, the tsar's preternatural detachment, which had always been part of his appeal, stood out as a negative and inhuman trait.

I rushed to Sochi as quickly as I could. It wasn't clear to me either, at first, why Putin had not gone to the scene immediately.

"What do you want me to do?" he complained. "They're all dead. It's obvious. We can't say it yet because we haven't reached them, but that's obviously what's happened. Berezovsky's whole circus is just that: a circus."

It was true, no question. Berezovsky had raised the big tent, erected the spectator stands, and now he was waiting for Putin to come down and exhibit himself in the arena. The tsar, bridling at the prospect of playing the wild beast brought to heel, had no intention of giving him that satisfaction. "Tell them I don't want to get in the way of the rescue operations," he told his spokesman. And that was the version of events we had to peddle to the outside world. But it didn't work, it was an overly rational argument in answer to an outburst of hysteria. Did Putin really not know this?

One night, it must have been the second or third day into the crisis, we were watching the nightly newscast. The tsar made it a point of honor to follow the televised news even during normal times, and on these days he hadn't missed a single broadcast. After the usual segments on the navy's ineptness, Putin's unexplained absence, the shocked reaction of foreigners, and the despair of the crew's close family members, the news anchor turned toward the camera: "In view of the government's inaction," he said, "ORT has decided to establish a fund to benefit the families of the sailors. If you'd like to send help to the loved ones of the heroes abandoned to their fate by the Russian government, call this number." Putin exploded with rage.

"Do you realize what's happening, Vadya? The same people who've spent the last ten years destroying the state, who've robbed us blind, who've put our army on the breadline, now have the gall to organize a fund for the families of the victims! A benefit fund! Maybe those hypocrites should give up their chalets in Saint Moritz first! Get that son of a bitch on the phone for me, call him on his cell!"

He didn't need to explain who he was talking about. For a time, Berezovsky listened quietly while

Putin harangued him angrily and indignantly. I could almost see Boris sprawled on a poolside deck chair, his face wearing the expression of a self-satisfied Persian cat. Eventually he spoke: "But Volodya, tell me just one thing: Why are you on the shores of the Black Sea? You should be at the scene, coordinating operations. Or else in Moscow."

Blind with rage, the tsar shot back: "And what about you, Boris, why are you on the Côte d'Azur?"

—Come on, Volodya, I'm not the president. No one gives a fuck where I am.

He was right. But as often happens, it didn't help him.

—Do you realize, Boris, that as we speak your station is airing interviews with prostitutes who've been paid to play the part of the sailors' wives and sisters? You run the state television and you're conspiring against the office of the president? Have you lost your mind?

At the other end of the line, Berezovsky now became agitated too. "What are you talking about? Those aren't actresses, Volodya, they're real women! You'd know that if you went and talked to them instead of listening to your cronies at the FSB!"

The conversation continued in this vein for some time, until Boris changed his tune: if Putin would attend the meeting of the sailors' parents, he said, ORT would guarantee the president favorable coverage.

The idea of Berezovsky dictating his actions was highly distasteful to the tsar. But what could he do under the circumstances? Suddenly, it seemed that he was the one lying in a steel sarcophagus at the bottom of the ocean. And the only person who could raise him to the surface was Boris.

When he put the receiver down, the tsar's face was as pale as a wax mask.

"We'll go to Moscow and arrange this fucking meeting," he said quietly. "And once this little situation is behind us, we'll take care of your friend."

14

ONE OF ISAAC BABEL'S stories, based on his war experiences, is called "My First Goose." It's about a young Jew on his first day in the Red Army during the 1920 campaign. He's just arrived, and his barracks mates, illiterate Cossacks, start picking on him because of his glasses and his intellectual air. One of them gets up, and without a word, tosses his trunk into the street, then turns his back and makes mocking sounds. Does the young man whine or complain? No, instead he catches a goose that is waddling peacefully around, steps on its head with his hobnailed boot, impales it on the tip of his sword, and carries it to the cook who hadn't wanted to serve him dinner. "Roast this for me," he says. From that moment on, of course, the Cossacks welcome him in their midst. The little Jew may wear glasses, but he's a good fellow deep down and he's shown that he has grit.

Berezovsky was my first goose. My background
was in theater, my father was an intellectual, and I had
to show the Cossacks I wasn't a weakling. Taking away
Boris's television station was easy enough to do. Berezovsky didn't own a majority interest in ORT, only 49
percent. The rest belonged to the state. All I had to do
was call the station's CEO and tell him that he'd be
taking his instructions from the Kremlin from now on,
not from Logovaz.

—Wasn't that a little brutal?

—Well, as the old saying goes: the executioner's
mercy lies in the deftness of his stroke. It's true that
Boris didn't take it very well. The executives at ORT
stopped taking his calls from one day to the next. His
star reporter was fired point-blank. Even the young
lovelies who worked as hostesses at the Novokuznetskaya clubhouse couldn't get airtime anymore. Berezovsky went crazy. He started unleashing a flood of
harsh invective on anyone and everyone. And as Putin
didn't answer his calls, he'd call me up instead to vent
his anger, laying every kind of misdeed at my door,
including some I hadn't committed.

This was all perfectly normal. Anyone would have
done the same in his place. But Berezovsky wasn't just
anyone. Which is why, rather than accept defeat, he
made a fatal mistake: he called a press conference to
denounce the administration for its abuse of power
and warn that Russia was becoming an authoritarian
state. He went in front of the cameras to yammer about

freedom of the press and the violation of human rights as if he were Solzhenitsyn. But the public saw him for what he was—an unscrupulous wheeler-dealer scrabbling to hold on to the power he'd lost because of the political rise of the tsar.

Berezovsky was extremely bright, but he hadn't studied history. Otherwise he'd have known that the rules of power, unlike the laws of nature, are subject to change. The rise of the oligarchs occurred during a sort of feudal interval after the fall of the Soviet regime. Boris and the others had become the pillars of a system in which the Kremlin was substantially dependent on them, with their money, their newspapers, and their television stations. When the oligarchs decided to give Putin their backing, they thought they were choosing a new representative, not changing the whole system. They took the tsar's election as a modest event, whereas it was the start of a new epoch. An epoch during which their role was going to be redefined.

Anyone who knows Russia knows that power in our country is periodically subject to tectonic shifts. Before the fact, you might try to alter its course. Afterwards, all the many interlocking parts of society become realigned according to a silent and implacable logic. To rebel against these shifts would be as useless as to oppose the earth's rotation around the sun.

Berezovsky and the other oligarchs liked to present themselves as pillars of democracy, and they expected people to go to the barricades to defend them. But they overestimated how popular they were. We, on the other hand, had a pretty good idea. If you look at Aristotle, you'll see that according to him, a demagogue's first action on coming to power is to banish all oligarchs. People regarded Boris and his ilk as profiteers who'd siphoned off vast quantities of the accumulated wealth of the Soviet Union using brutal measures. Then, once they'd stockpiled their mountains of cash, taken off their bulletproof vests, and put on a custom-tailored suit, they announced that the time for brutality was over, that all would now be fair play and House of Lords rules. It makes sense, really, that so many of them chose London as their place of exile. That's where Berezovsky headed when he finally understood how badly he'd misjudged the situation.

I went to see him at Logovaz House for a last visit shortly before he left. The tsar had asked me to let him know he still considered him a friend. "Make sure he understands that he's got to steer clear of politics from now on," he said. "If he does that, he can stay quietly in Moscow to run his businesses as far as I'm concerned. Or he can sail to the other side of the world. But if he dabbles in politics, he'll always find us blocking his path."

Few things are sadder than an abandoned seat of power where the ghosts of the past have assumed a stronger presence than the flesh-and-blood men who linger on.

When I went to Logovaz House, Berezovsky was already practically alone. I conveyed the tsar's message in the friendliest terms I could find, but he still didn't take it very well. He tried at first to restrain himself, but as the conversation progressed he gave voice to the rage that had been building in him for months.

"Putin is a chekist, Vadya, a chekist of the worst kind, the kind that neither smokes nor drinks. They're the worst because their vices are hidden. He'll put Russia in chains. Everything we've done in the past few years to become a normal country will go to ruin. You too, Vadya, sooner or later. But come to think of it, you already wear a collar, you're the chekist's lapdog. Just like your father. It's in your blood, that aptitude for submission. Call yourselves aristocrats? You're serfs through and through, and you've been serfs for generations!"

His words washed over me leaving no trace, like a mountain stream over a rock. It occurred to me idly that Custine would have thought he was right. Too bad Boris had never read the man, he'd have found him useful. He plowed ahead, contradicting himself as he went.

"But you're not going to get away with it, Vadya. Think of the Europeans, the Americans, they won't allow it. Russians have had a taste of democracy now. There will be a civil war..."

His mention of a civil war made me laugh. As a French diplomat once said, the advantage of a civil war over the other kind is that you can go home for meals.

"Right, Vadya, laugh on." Boris was becoming more and more agitated. "You people are setting up a regime that's even worse than the Soviet Union. At least in those days, the KGB watchdogs were kept in check by the people in the Communist Party. Now the party no longer exists, and the chekists are in power. Who is going to curb their arrogance, their greed, their profound stupidity? Are you going to do it, Vadya? Or your theater friends? The KGB without the Communist Party is nothing but a gang of crooks!"

I stopped myself from reminding Berezovsky of our first meeting with Putin at the Lubyanka. It had been his obliviousness that led us to recruit a successor to Yeltsin in the dark corners of that sinister prison. I wasn't particularly disturbed by his insults, but his complete lack of good faith was starting to get on my nerves.

"At least we have the press and the media," he said. "They've grown used to being free. They're not going to let you take that away from them, believe me."

"Wait a minute," I said. "Wasn't it you who was telling us that a journalist can be bought and sold for a handful of change? That he's a house servant who has been given permission to sit with you? That if you read one or two of his editorials, he'll puff up like a peacock and fawn over you forever? Or am I wrong, Boris, was it someone else telling us that?"

I shouldn't have, I know. But patience has its limits. Boris abruptly clammed up as if he'd seen a ghost. It was actually his own reflection, the ghost of Berezovskys past. Which he knew. There was no point in dwelling on it.

He looked at me sorrowfully, suddenly showing his age. His season was over and would return no more. He could keep his money, yes. But he'd be one of those rich men that people pretend to listen to because they pick up the check at the end of the meal and nothing more. His opinions would have no further influence on the course of events.

"Well done, Vadya, you've become one of them," he said. "Did you keep some recordings to use against me? Sechin would already have played them for the tsar, are you going to do that too? It's all working out for you, at least so far. But you're not like them, and you never will be." Berezovsky's voice descended to a hate-filled hiss. "They're wild animals, Vadya. They've come out of the void, hacking a path with their war clubs. No rules, no limits. They're hungry, and their hunger is ancestral. They've suffered humiliation, centuries of humiliation. They have to have it all right away, because they know that the wheel is turning. But what do you know about it? For people like you, the wheel doesn't turn."

—Maybe so, Boris, I don't know. What I do know is that Russians have always forged their way ahead, swinging an axe.

Berezovsky gave me a worried look. The show was over, and he knew it better than anyone. The one thing left to do was to stand up and walk away. There was a melancholy dignity in the way the old actor gave his final bow. Those were my thoughts, at any rate, as I left Logovaz House for the last time.

15

POLITICS IS A STRANGE business. If you make it your career, you have to maintain close ties with your base. Keep tabs on what the housewives want, the railway workers, the small business owners. Then when you get to the top, you're flung onto the global stage. The world's great players are suddenly your peers. And they already have their little gang, because they've been around for a while, they've had a chance to get to know each other, learn the ropes. You, on the other hand, are just a novice, pushed onstage for a surprise performance. You might be respected or feared back in your own country, but here you're just the most recent arrival. You have to start over at zero and learn everything again, from how to walk to how to return a greeting. The G8 summits, the UN assemblies, the Davos forums—each has its own rituals. Your new friends are amiable enough, each appearing eager to give you a hand. But don't be fooled. Each has worked out a plan to fuck you over.

While Berezovsky was flying to London, we were headed in the opposite direction: first to Tokyo, then to New York. At JFK, we were met by our UN ambassador at the foot of the plane, with a squadron of limos and black SUVs, led by a police car. On the road into the city, we moved at a snail's pace, stopping at every red light. A siren would occasionally sound when a distracted motorist edged into our motorcade, but there was no display of the imperious hierarchy that marks power in Moscow. When we reached the Waldorf Astoria, we realized that the hotel was hosting several other delegations as well as ours. The Kremlin's Office of Protocol had reserved twenty rooms for us, but above our heads the Saudis occupied the top three floors in lavish splendor.

The week of the United Nations General Assembly is a power orgy, but also a lesson in humility. Men who are used to having their desires satisfied instantly must relearn the virtues that come from waiting. The processions of armored cars and bodyguards make for interminable bottlenecks on Second Avenue; testosterone-charged delegations clash together in the crowded hallways of the Glass House; heads of state who are used to elegant drawing rooms find themselves huddling behind temporary screens to conduct crucial negotiations. And with all this, of course, the Americans always find a way to make you aware of their superiority.

One day we were leaving the hotel for an appointment at CNN when a Secret Service agent made us stop. "It's the Freeze," he explained. "When the president is on the move, everyone else has to freeze in place." I can still remember the tsar's expression while he waited on the sidewalk for our delegation to get the all clear to start moving again. But when we reached the television station, we were greeted by a kind of circus performer whose face was familiar. Pink shirt, black suspenders. Standing next to Larry King, the tsar looked like he was dressed for his first communion.

"So what's it like to be a spy?" the guy asked him during the broadcast.

—Not so different from being a journalist, said Putin. You gather information, make a synthesis, and present it to someone else, who will use it to make decisions.

—So, you enjoyed doing that?

—On the whole I did. Working in information allowed me to broaden my vision and develop a number of people skills. I learned to tell the difference between what's a priority and what's less important, and in that sense it's been very useful to me.

—Great! We'll be back with President Putin on *Larry King Live* after this break, don't go away!

At the time, we were still taking it all very seriously, but New York is such a carnival that we let ourselves go a bit. I've always thought of Manhattan as the grid of a board game where the players come and go by subway, yellow cab, or black town car, according to their rank. The city is devoid of wisdom, doomed to endless repetition, but bursting with energy. Our motorcade had none of its Moscow majesty, but it made an impression all the same. We'd be at a gallery opening and go from there to a gala dinner. And everywhere we were greeted with that expansive American cordiality, which almost always hides a trace of condescension.

The summit with President Clinton followed the same general format. The president kindly came to the Waldorf to meet us. He acted the part of the grizzled political veteran—his legendary handshake, where both his hands envelop yours like a boa constrictor, his hoarse voice, and the big smile of a Midwestern farmer who will sit by the fire after nightfall and tell you stories of his life. But we knew that the rustic exterior hid a sophisticated and implacable mechanism. Clinton the straight-A student at Yale and Oxford, Clinton the youngest governor in United States history, Clinton the political animal who managed to survive every political scandal and always triumphed over his adversaries in the end. Clinton, above all, who with an iron hand presided over the dismantling of the Soviet Empire, took back half of Europe without conceding anything in return, expanded NATO almost to our borders, and let the vultures dismember piece by piece what was left of our industrial system.

Nonetheless, he made a mistake in his opening exchange with Putin. He asked the tsar for news of Yeltsin, his old friend Boris. What he didn't realize is that he was reactivating the memory of a humiliation none of us could ever quite put behind us. Russians, as I've said before, are used to making sacrifices, but they're also accustomed to getting respect. All through our history, Russian rulers have been treated as great world figures, and no one has ever lorded it over them. When Roosevelt met with Stalin, or in later decades, Nixon met with Brezhnev or Reagan with Gorbachev, two great powers came face-to-face, and no one would ever have thought otherwise. After the fall of the Berlin Wall, all that became more problematic, though a simple respect for the formalities could have saved us. But Yeltsin fell into the trap of Clinton's backslapping, good-old-boy heartiness, convinced he'd found a friend. Or at least an ally who was well disposed toward him and who'd help him put Russia back on its feet. So he lowered his guard. After accepting a handshake, then a pat on the back, he found himself caught up in the horrible sequence of events that has seared itself into the retina of every Russian as a mark of shame.

Try to imagine the scene: it's an autumn day, once again in New York. The presidents of Russia and the United States have just concluded a bilateral agreement at the Franklin D. Roosevelt Library, and they are now standing outside it for a joint press conference.

Neoclassical columns, national flags, presidential guards in dress uniform, and, at the foot of the podium, two pumpkins in honor of the barbaric celebration that Americans have, as usual, managed to inflict on the rest of the world. Clinton speaks briefly, then turns the microphone over to Yeltsin, who, clearly not sober, starts to harangue the crowd. While our president's voice rings out, Clinton bursts out laughing. It's unusual, but it's no big deal. Even the most powerful man in the world sometimes has to laugh. The problem is that Clinton doesn't stop. He can't help himself. The old Russian bear, staggering and ridiculous, convulses the American president, doubles him over with laughter. Clinton has tears in his eyes, his face has turned a deep red, and his laughing jag is out of control. Glued to the television, we Russians are silently begging Clinton to stop. We know Yeltsin, his habits, his failings. But he's the president of the Russian Federation, for Christ's sake, the largest country on the planet, a nuclear superpower! But no, Clinton can't hold it in. Now he's staggering too, giving Yeltsin great claps on the back. Yeltsin, even in his tipsy state, starts to look somewhat aggrieved. An entire nation, a hundred and fifty million Russians, is dragged down in embarrassment by the weight of the American president's laughter.

This is the scene that flashed through the tsar's mind when Clinton asked him about old Boris. Straight off, he let Clinton know things would be different with him. No more slapping on the back and howling with laughter. Clinton was obviously disappointed. He thought that all Russian presidents going forward would be obliging hotel doormen, guarding the largest reserves of natural gas on the planet for American multinational corporations. For once, Clinton and his advisors left with a smaller smile on their faces than when they'd arrived. But what did they expect?

"If cannibals came to power in Moscow," said the tsar on the flight home, "the United States would immediately recognize them as the legitimate government, as long as they didn't interfere with American interests and continued to treat the U.S. as the boss. The problem is that they think they've won the Cold War. But the Soviet Union didn't lose it. The Cold War stopped because the Russian people overthrew a regime that was oppressing them. We weren't beaten, we freed ourselves from a dictatorship. Two different things. The West also helped democratize Eastern Europe, but they shouldn't forget that it was the Russians who really tipped the balance. We made the Berlin Wall fall, not they. We dissolved the Warsaw Pact. And we held out our hand to them as a sign of peace, not surrender. It would be nice if they remembered this from time to time."

16

WHEN WE RETURNED FROM the United States, I decided to go out for a night on the town. Although I no longer had much free time, I would occasionally visit the watering holes of the Moscow art crowd, which I'd mostly avoided since I started working for the tsar. Irritated as I was by the nervous tics they affected to give themselves importance, I found the artists' forced gaiety a welcome relief from the unrelenting and predatory vigilance of my colleagues at the Kremlin. Notable in the crowd was a character who displayed all the affectations of a great writer without ever having taken the trouble to write a book of corresponding stature. This was Limonov, Eduard Limonov. After spending many years in America and Paris, he had returned to Moscow with combative ideas. He cultivated a fierce resentment toward the West, fanned by the humiliations he had endured there, which were mostly of a pecuniary nature. In the early 1990s, he created the National Bolshevik Party. It wasn't entirely clear whether this was a political operation or performance art, but it was unquestionably intended to create a maximum of chaos. Having long ago divested himself of the irksome benefits of respectability, to which I and others still clung, Eduard had access to an infinite range of more intense pleasures. These he shared with his close circle, displaying the generosity of a Middle Eastern pasha. He was always surrounded by an unlikely cast of characters that he called "my revolutionary avant-garde."

"Laugh all you want, Vadya, but I'm creating an army," he said. "The problem isn't the soldiers, they're in plentiful enough supply—people are so desperate. No, the problem is finding the political commissars, the ones who are capable of generating propaganda, of speaking to the masses. At this stage in the struggle, they are the strategic weapon, the propagators of ideology, the multipliers of the National Bolshevik revolution. But don't worry, Vadya, when we take over, we'll let you keep your little office in the Kremlin—a bona fide propaganda professional can always come in handy..."

That evening, Eduard had offered to meet me at 317, a faux Irish pub near the White House that served as his headquarters. To reach it, you had to thread your way through the dozens of motorbikes parked outside. The ambience was full-on *Mad Max*, with neofascist bikers cheek by jowl with anarchist intellectuals, punks, and the few women who dared venture inside.

When I arrived, Limonov was already seated at a corner table with a half-empty bottle of vodka in front of him—a promising start to the evening.

"Do you know what marked the beginning of the end, Vadya?" Eduard always liked to start a conversation dramatically.

"No, Eduard. Please enlighten me."

—Richelieu, Vadya. He was the cardinal in *The Three Musketeers*, but he actually existed in real life, did you know?

—Yes, Eduard, let me remind you that you're not addressing one of your brain-dead skinheads.

—OK, right. Anyway, it was he who outlawed dueling. He passed a law that forbade two adult males from challenging each other to a sword fight, can you imagine? Western man has never recovered. From there to paid paternity leave was just a small step.

Limonov considered paid paternity leave, which had just been introduced in several European countries, to be abjectly degrading to man's status, the symbol of his demotion to domestic animal.

"They watch television, park the car, work at some undemanding but totally boring job. A few decades slip by, they get a loan or two, take a vacation on the beach, and then their life is over, before they've even realized it. A total waste of a life, the one truly unforgivable crime."

I'd heard Eduard's arguments a number of times already. They were the same ones he rehearsed in his books, his interviews, and his speeches to the members of his revolutionary avant-garde. That night, however, he was curious about our trip to New York, which he'd read about in the newspapers.

"How was your junket to the States?" he asked.

I tried to sidestep the conversation, not wanting to discuss international affairs with Eduard. "Oh, you know what it's like over there," I said. "Actually, it's always quite a lot of fun."

—Yes, New York is fun. As long as you avoid Americans.

I laughed, but as usual he was serious. Although he was constantly spinning paradoxes, Limonov never joked. It was one of his traits.

"Have you ever been to one of those dinners?" he asked. "All the men are graduates of Princeton or Yale, all the women of Vassar or Brown. Their children are all the same age and go to the same schools. The men work in a bank downtown, the women shop at Barneys. They all have a summer house in the Hamptons and a winter house in Palm Beach. If you're stuck at one of those tables, cyanide is the only viable option. When I was younger, I could at least try to charm one of the blonde wives. Now cyanide is my only recourse. But luckily, I'm not invited to those dinners anymore."

—What can you do, old man, the discreet charm of the bourgeoisie. It's the same all over.

—No, Vadya, America has destroyed the bourgeoisie.

The chief ideologue of the National Bolshevik Party suddenly assumed an expression of deep sorrow, lamenting the disappearance of the Anglo-Saxon bourgeoisie.

—The bourgeoisie at least had values, whereas these people believe only in numbers. What's funny is that they don't even know each other, they're the product of a lottery that starts over with each generation— intelligent and ambitious, worshipful of work and exact data, they're as dull as dead rats. The problem isn't the United States' imperialism. I'm not angry over what they did to Allende or any of their other shenanigans. The exercise of power, even the violent exercise of power, is part and parcel of any empire, and at the end of the day the U.S. is no worse than many of its predecessors, including our white and red tsarevitches. The problem is the content of American culture—a decline from civilization that has put true greatness out of reach so as to guarantee everyone a Happy Meal.

Eduard paused a moment to chomp the hamburger he'd ordered, without disturbing the thread of his argument in the least.

—What's interesting is that people like you think it's a model that should be copied. But the truth is that Americans are zombies. There's no greater sin than frittering your life away, Vadya. They don't have the remotest notion that the goal of human existence might be something other than to live as long as possible in as much comfort as possible. When I saw that Yeltsin was going down that road, that he wanted to turn Russia into a low-rent spin-off of the American hospice, that's when I decided to found the National Bolshevik Party. And do you know why I gave it that name? To rattle your cages, to squeeze into one name everything you think is evil, all the ideas that threaten the happy little consumer you've reduced man to.

—"Passion makes a man live, wisdom only makes him last."

Limonov glared at me. He didn't like to be interrupted, least of all by a literary quotation that trivialized his insight.

"That's the whole idea," he said. "The National Bolshevik Party brought together ex-Stalinists and ex-Trotskyites, gays and skinheads, anarchists, punks, conceptual artists and religious fanatics, Buddhists and Orthodox Christians. When we held our first conference, the hardest part was to figure out how to seat everyone so they wouldn't crack each other's skulls. Looking back on it, I still don't know how we managed…"

Eduard burst out laughing. Then, steadied by a swig of vodka, he grew serious again.

"It wasn't ideology that brought them together under one tent, Vadya, it was lifestyle. You think our

platform interested them in the slightest? What these
youngsters want is a release from triviality, to escape
from boredom. There's a spark of heroism in each of
them just waiting to be fed. The Third Rome, imperial
Russia, Stalingrad, it doesn't matter! The main thing
is to summon greatness. To avoid extinction, every
people needs to believe that it holds the key to the
world's salvation, that it exists to take the head of the
line—ahead of all other nations! The Western world
wants to see us on our knees. They loved Gorbachev
and Yeltsin. They'll pretend to love you too, Vadya, as
long as you maintain the posture of a valet. Meanwhile,
they'll carry off anything that's not nailed down."

I made a point that night not to tell Limonov that
his thinking coincided, at least in part, with what our
experiences in the United States had taught us. It worried me, actually. I'd always thought of Eduard as a
brilliant sociopath, but with no sense of politics at all.
He'd been hammering away at the same ideas for years
to amuse his friends. And to scandalize bourgeois sen-
sibility, to draw attention to himself, and make the
young lovelies, always well represented in his entou-
rage, open their eyes wide as saucers—this had always
seemed the sole aim of his tirades. Now, however, I
was starting to draw a different meaning from his out-
bursts. It hadn't reached the point where I would say
that he was right, far from it. But for the first time,
his arguments struck me for what they were. Not a
product of rigorous analysis, but nonetheless an insight

that wasn't to be taken lightly, despite all of Limonov's clowning. Maybe the frenzied imitation of the West that we'd thrown ourselves into during the late 1990s was not the right path. Maybe the moment had come to take a different route.

17

IT WAS THAT HOUR of night when death comes into the world, and I felt, as I walked the long white halls of the Kremlin, that I was in the only place in Russia not sunk in total darkness. The Senate Palace, which houses Putin's office, has none of the icy grandeur of the palace of the tsars. Power does not glide over the mirrors of useless drawing rooms there and disperse, but comes to a head, instead, and takes action. Lenin made it the seat of his government for this reason, and the fate of the most gigantic country on earth has ever since been decided in these small, perfunctorily furnished rooms.

Arriving in the president's antechamber, I nodded my usual greeting to the portraits of the tsars and the statue of the Japanese samurai that Putin had picked to reinforce the flesh-and-blood youths of his security guard. The chief of staff waved me through; the president was expecting me. As the door closed behind me, I found him seated at his worktable rather than on the couch where he normally chose to conduct our private conversations. Bad sign. The big bronze chandelier had for once been turned off. Only the tsar's desk was lit by a small lamp, creating an atmosphere of studious reflection. I sat in one of the two awkward armchairs facing his desk.

The tsar was reading a document and said nothing for several minutes. Then, without lifting his eyes from the sheet in front of him, he spoke: "Where are my approval ratings, Vadya?"

—At approximately sixty percent, Mister President.

—Right. And do you know who's ahead of me?

—There's no one, sir. Your nearest rival is at about twelve percent.

—Not true, Vadya. Think again, there's a Russian leader who's more popular than I am.

I had no idea what he was talking about.

"Stalin is more popular at this moment than I am. If we were to go head-to-head in an election, Russia's 'Little Father' would trounce me!"

The tsar's face had assumed a stony consistency that I had learned to recognize. I refrained from making any comment.

"You intellectuals think it's because people have forgotten. You think they don't remember the purges, the massacres. That's why you keep publishing book after book, and article after article, on the events of

1937, on the gulags, on the victims of Stalinism. You think Stalin is popular in spite of the massacres. Well you're wrong, he's popular *because* of the massacres. Because at least he knew how to deal with thieves and traitors."

The tsar paused.

"Do you know what Stalin did when there was an uptick in Soviet train wrecks?"

—No.

—He took von Meck, the man in charge of railroads, and had him executed for sabotage. It didn't resolve the railroad problem, in fact it may have made it worse. But it provided an outlet for anger. The same thing happened each time the system fell short. When meat grew scarce, Stalin arrested the people's commissar for agriculture, Chernov. When they tried him, lo and behold, Chernov confessed that he'd had thousands of cows and pigs slaughtered in order to destabilize the government and incite rebellion. Then there was a shortage of butter and eggs. So Stalin had Zelensky arrested, the man in charge of distributing consumer products. And it didn't take long for Zelensky to admit that he'd mixed nails and ground glass into the butter supply and had fifty truckloads of eggs destroyed. There was a wave of indignation across the country, mixed with relief: it could all be explained! And Vadya, sabotage is a much more convincing explanation than inefficiency. Once you've found the culprit, you can punish him. Justice has prevailed. Someone has had to pay, and order has been restored. That's the crucial point.

The tsar paused again, in a way that in other circumstances I'd have called theatrical. Then he continued in a neutral voice: "I've given orders to have your old friend Khodorkovsky arrested at dawn tomorrow. We'll send cameras along too—that way everyone will see that nobody, absolutely nobody, is above the sacred anger of the Russian people."

I was astonished. Over the last several years, Mikhail had become the wealthiest entrepreneur in the country. He wasn't necessarily more honest than the rest, but he had a straight-arrow image and a nerdish, Silicon Valley vibe—T-shirts, wire-framed glasses, a nonprofit humanitarian aid foundation, and big speeches full of noble ideals. Your newspapers and television adored him, turned him into a kind of icon of the new Russian capitalism. The idea of tossing him in jail like a common criminal was practically inconceivable. But it was true the tsar hadn't gotten where he was by sticking to the realm of the conceivable.

I never thought for a minute that the tsar's order was anything but irrevocable. The man looking at me from across the desk hadn't asked my advice, he had simply communicated his decision. My job was to manage the consequences. The media, even in Russia, would play it up as scandalous. We could have soft-pedaled the arrest, presented it as some kind of administrative order, but it wouldn't have solved anything.

At this point we might as well double down on it. If Mikhail was to become the outlet for the Russian people's anger, his humiliation had to be complete. Enough with the photographs of the golden boy of finance, the smiling benefactor of widows and orphans. I was going to see to it that from now on the only images in circulation would be ones that showed Khodorkovsky in prison garb and behind bars. The message had to be clear: you went from the cover of *Forbes* straight to jail if that's what the tsar wanted. Mikhail's public cashiering would be a warning to other oligarchs and a spectacle served up to the Russian people to appease their wrath.

You may think that I had some personal animus in carrying out this business, that I took pleasure in humiliating my old rival, but I can assure you that's not true. The moment you choose to get revenge for a wrong you've suffered, you become its hostage. I'd freed myself long before of any thought of Mikhail and Ksenia, to the point where even the news of their marriage didn't disturb my equanimity. It was unpleasant having to revisit the episode, but it would have made no sense to object. Nothing's harder than coming to a decision, but once you've done it, everything else has to be set aside except what will bring it to fruition.

Khodorkovsky was arrested at dawn, the moment his jet touched down in the Siberian town where he'd gone to conduct some now-forgotten business. Images of the handcuffed billionaire under special forces guard traveled around the world. And had the immediate effect of reminding people that money doesn't protect you from everything. This is absolutely taboo to you Westerners. A politician can be arrested, why not; but a billionaire, that's inconceivable, because your society is based on the principle that nothing is greater than money. What's funny is that you keep calling wealthy Russians "oligarchs," when the truth is that the only real oligarchs are in the West. That's where billionaires stand above the law and above the people, that's where they buy government officials and write laws in their stead. In your part of the world, the idea of Bill Gates, of Rupert Murdoch, of Mark Zuckerberg in handcuffs is unthinkable. Whereas in Russia, a billionaire is perfectly free to spend his money, but not to influence politics. The will of the Russian people—and of the tsar, who is its incarnation—counts for more than any private interest.

Occurring just six weeks before the election, Khodorkovsky's arrest served as the leitmotif for the tsar's noncampaign. My role was limited to reformatting Mikhail's fall into good television. It wasn't hard. The head of a powerful man rolling on the ground is a spectacle that the masses always appreciate. When a big shot is put to death, the multitude is consoled for its own mediocrity. I may not have been all that successful, says the man on the street, but at least I'm not up there on the hangman's scaffold. Public executions have been highly prized in every age. The first time a guillotine was used, the chronicles of the French Revolution report, Parisians complained of not being able to see, and called for the return of the headman's axe. But when they realized how effective the guillotine was and how terrifying to the condemned, they started to see the appeal of the new technology. Let's just face it: the people are more bloodthirsty than any dictator; only the leader's stern but fair intercession can temper their fury.

The election, held in early December, was a great victory. The following day, the tsar confessed on television that he had been up all night. Not to follow the election results, about which he never had any doubt, but because his Labrador retriever, Koni, had given birth to her first litter. I had no dog, so I was at home on election night, alone with a carafe of vodka and a pile of history books. After my last conversation with the tsar, I had started to see my role differently. I'd been burrowing into accounts of the Stalinist trials of the 1930s and begun to realize that these were already big-budget Hollywood extravaganzas—show business in the Soviet style. The prosecutor and the judges worked for months on the screenplay, which the defendants were then called on to act out, with the producers pressuring them in various ways. Some had a family to protect, others a secret to keep hidden, while others might quite simply be susceptible to threats or physical pain. Eventually, everyone would agree to play their role, and the show could start.

No detail escaped the producers' attention, the mix of reality and fiction had to be impeccable. The public, those allowed to attend the trial in person, but more especially the millions who stayed home and followed the trial on the radio and in the pages of *Pravda*, experienced the same range of emotions as watching a Metro-Goldwyn-Mayer epic—the fear, anguish, and horror we feel when confronted with pure Evil. Then the deep serenity that comes from the conflict's resolution and the victory of Good. There is no limit to the creative capacity of a government willing to act with the necessary determination, as long as it respects the basic rules pertaining to each narrative construct. The limit is determined not by the respect for truth, but by the respect for fiction. The primordial motive force in all this remains anger. You self-righteous Westerners think that anger can be absorbed, that all it takes is economic growth and technological progress, along with affordable home delivery and mass tourism, to dissipate the people's wrath, the silent, sacrosanct anger of the people, whose roots reach deep into the very origins of humanity. It isn't true. There will always be people who are disappointed, who are frustrated, who are on the losing end in every epoch and under every government. Stalin understood that anger is a structural given. At different times, it increases or decreases, but it never disappears. It's one of the undercurrents governing society. So the issue is not how to stop it but how to manage it. If it isn't to overrun its banks and destroy everything in its path, you constantly have to provide overflow channels. Situations where anger can go wild without putting the whole system in danger. Repressing dissidence is a crude tactic. Managing the flow of anger so that it doesn't accumulate is more difficult, but it's also much more effective. For many years, basically, that was my job.

18

AFTER KHODORKOVSKY'S ARREST AND Putin's runaway reelection, the Russian government underwent a change. The struggle for power didn't end, not in the least. But it moved out of the public arena and into the tsar's antechamber. From then on, it was the court that again determined what happened to the state. And the sovereign's brow, as in the time of Nicholas I, was again the source of all the joys and sorrows of his courtiers.

If you ever have the opportunity to visit a zoo, watch the lions and the monkeys. When they are playing, it means that the hierarchies are clearly drawn and the leader securely in control. In the opposite case, each animal goes to its corner, jittery and afraid. By reestablishing the power vertical, Putin sounded the strains that set the courtiers' dance in motion—an exercise in dexterity whose rules go back to the far depths of time and whose rhythm is determined by the upward and downward movements of the participants. Some have offices close to the tsar's, and some are on his direct telephone line. Some are included on visits to foreign nations, while others go to Sochi on vacation. Some find themselves with a seat in government, others are not reappointed to lead a public company. No indication, however small, can afford to be overlooked: the seating arrangement at a gala dinner, the wait time in the president's antechamber, the number of agents in one's security detail. Power is made up of minutiae. Nothing escapes the obsessive interest of the courtier, because he knows that the essence of hierarchy lies in the details. And that even a tiny loss of control can cause a crack in the edifice. Only dilettantes neglect these clues, dismissing them as unworthy of their attention. The professional knows that no detail is too small.

The Kremlin has many towers, and oscillations occur constantly, so whoever wants to stay in the game has to measure these oscillations with the precision of a seismograph from the Moscow Geophysical Institute. An exhausting undertaking, requiring continuous attention. Every encounter, whether in public or in private, serves to take the pulse of the current moment, to check that the balance of powers is unchanged. Do you know the strip of stock quotes continuously scrolling above the trading floor? That's what the Kremlin's court is like. Except that instead of being posted on a screen, the quotes are on the foreheads and lips of the courtiers. Every dinner, every conversation, becomes a stock market listing: who's up, who's down. And every player who's at all serious knows that the Kremlin doesn't offer happiness, but it does make it impossible to be happy anywhere else.

For my part, and I don't deny it, I settled into the Kremlin's new order easily, as befits a person with three centuries of bowing and scraping in his bloodline. Admittedly there were others who, though lacking my genetic inheritance, managed to surpass me all the same. Sechin, for instance, Putin's secretary. I've mentioned him before, he was someone who opened doors, made phone calls, and for a long time, like many men of his type, derived his strength from being underestimated. People would see him there, with his little attaché case, staring at the floor whenever the tsar was near, and they assumed he was part typist and part personal butler. In four years at the Kremlin, he became the archetype courtier, sure of himself and dominating; the world was his as long as the tsar was not around. But let the tsar throw a glance his way, and he turned back into a quivering lamb.

On government flights, when everyone else took off their jackets to be more comfortable, he kept his tie knotted as a sign of respect to the tsar. Before meeting Putin, he'd worked for the KGB in Mozambique. God knows what he did there, but from time to time he would go back. Disembarking from an Antonov transport on an African runway with a special forces escort and a message from the tsar for the local dictator was a kind of vacation to him. During the day, mortar fire marked the passing hours. At night, you'd eat by the pool while an orchestra played cocktail music. Like going to Capri or Saint-Tropez for a normal person.

His approach to human nature was so primitive that more sophisticated men had trouble understanding it. "The situation is more complicated than that," they'd tell him. "Balls" was Sechin's retort. And the facts almost always proved him right.

One day, I discovered that he had a degree in philology, and I had the absurd idea that we might have interests in common. When I got the chance, I tried to ask him about his favorite authors. We were in his office: "I haven't read a book since the day I earned my degree," he said in a monotone. "Just these." And he pointed to a stack of memos without headings, written by the security services.

In every transaction, there are tasks that no one wants to perform but that everyone needs done; that's where Sechin comes in. Now that Khodorkovsky was in jail, there was the problem of what to do with his company, Yukos. The liberals in the government wanted to let Mikhail keep it, but it was clear that the tsar's purpose went beyond punishing a single individual: the whole system had to be dismantled. Also, Yukos was the premier Russian company. The most admired. The wealthiest. A war prize to entice the appetite of the fiercest animals in the Kremlin.

Sechin gobbled it up in one mouthful. A court-ordered confiscation, a public auction with a single bidder, and Yukos ended up in the portfolio of a public conglomerate to which Igor had been named president a few months earlier. Your newspapers were outraged and declared that it was theft. But the story is a little more complicated. Sechin is a *silovik*, a "strongman" who graduated from the security services. They've always been crucial in Russia, strongmen: as soldiers, spies, policemen. And Sechin, because of his closeness to the tsar, has become their go-to. Now, it's clear that you in the West, living hypocritically, think that power, vigor, force, are a bit archaic. You believe in rules, with your lawyers communicating by certified mail and earning million-dollar fees. You love the annual get-togethers in Davos, the OECD, the superstar architects who build skyscrapers in Rotterdam and Beijing, and the chefs who open gourmet bistros in Bali and Zermatt. The idea of wearing a necktie makes you uncomfortable, it's become the mark of a subordinate, of a hotel concierge, a counter agent at the car rental. So when it comes to the uniform of a soldier or a policeman, it belongs in a museum, something for children to look at on school trips.

Then again, I was like you. I'd spent too much time reading your journals and sipping cappuccinos. Yukos's dismantlement struck me as barbarous, a throwback to the old customs that we'd tried to leave behind. God knows I wasn't fond of Khodorkovsky, but the idea that he would be replaced by a chekist was a chilling thought.

One night, Putin called me into his office. It was during the critical days when we had to make a decision about the fate of the company. The tsar was just back from a summit meeting abroad and so wired and exhausted that he couldn't bring himself to sit still but paced nervously around the room. "It's always the same story. They treat me as if I were president of Finland. Worse even, because at least Finland is a civilized country, whereas Russia is still half-savage, a drunken vagrant lurking by the door. Maybe they're right. We behaved like beggars first, giving everyone a big smile and making sure they saw the donations jar."

The tsar was silent for a moment, then he went on in quieter tones.

"When I was growing up in Leningrad, there were lots of homeless men on the streets. The neighborhood kids used to kick them. Just for the hell of it. And the more the street people protested, the more they got kicked. But there was one guy they left alone. He wasn't the biggest guy, in fact he was in pretty poor shape, I think his name was Stepan. But do you know what was different about him? He was crazy, completely unpredictable. If you went up to him, even to say hi, he might break a bottle over your head, just like that, for no reason. People told a lot of strange stories about him, they said he had certain powers, that he'd made people disappear. We'd see him from a distance, and when he started to smile it would scare us even more than when he yelled. We'd run away at top speed, and even the big guys in the neighborhood would take an alternate route to avoid running into Crazy Stipa. When you're down and out, the only weapon you have to protect your dignity is the ability to instill fear."

—The problem, Mister President, is that when we instill fear in our adversaries, we also instill fear in the markets. And that's something we cannot do.

Putin shuddered, and for the first time since I'd known him, I felt a glimmer of hatred directed at me.

"Get this one thing straight, Vadya, traders have never been in charge of Russia. Do you know why? Because they can't provide the two things that Russians require from the state: internal order and external power. Only twice, for two brief periods, have merchants governed our country: once for a few months after the Russian Revolution in 1917, before the Bolsheviks stepped in, and once for a few years after the fall of the Berlin Wall, during Yeltsin's time. And what happened? Chaos. An explosion of violence, the law of the jungle, wolves coming out of the forests and roaming our cities to devour the defenseless population."

The tsar's icy tones made the picture he was painting all the more terrifying.

"Your friend Khodorkovsky dressed like a Silicon Valley entrepreneur, but he was a wolf from the steppes. He never invented anything, he never created anything. He just helped himself to a piece of the Russian state, taking advantage of the weakness and corruption of the people who should have been protecting it. Do you know how much he paid for his oil concessions in 1995? Three hundred million dollars. And what their market value was two years later? Nine billion. What an amazing entrepreneur, no? What a genius! They're all the same, the oligarchs. All geniuses. And now they come to us and preach about respect for the law. And they finance our opponents because we're impolite, we don't listen to them enough. Maybe they'll replace me in a little while with someone who has a Harvard diploma, a puppet who'll make them look good at the Davos conference, what do you think?"

I, of course, thought nothing.

As he unburdened himself, the tsar's spirits rose. He went and sat behind his desk and waved me into the armchair across from him.

"We have to recover our sovereignty, Vadya. And the only way to do that is to mobilize all our resources. Our GDP is the size of Finland's? Maybe. But we're not Finland, we're the biggest country on earth. And the richest. Only we've allowed our wealth, the collective wealth that rightfully belongs to the Russian people, to be stolen by a bunch of bandits. In recent years, Russia has created an offshore aristocracy, people who hoard our resources but whose hearts and wallets are elsewhere. We'll take back control of the source of our country's wealth, Vadya: the gas, the oil, the forests, the mines, and we'll use these riches to further the interests and the greatness of the Russian people, not some gangster with a villa on the Costa del Sol.

"And there isn't just the economy. Take a look at the army. Yeltsin didn't know what to do with the military. He was partly afraid of it, partly contemptuous, so he avoided dealing with it and left it to rot far from the spotlights, the shop fronts, and the skyscrapers of the new Russia. That's how we became a kind of South American country, with generals who behave like gangsters and engage in politics, and soldiers who are dying of hunger and sell themselves for a pack of cigarettes. What we're doing now is to restore the army to the vertical of power, along with the security services. Force has always been at the heart of the Russian state, its raison d'être. But our duty is not simply to restore the power vertical, we need to create a new elite, a patriotic elite ready to go to any lengths to defend Russia's independence."

At the time, I still accepted what the tsar told me literally. I had no inkling of the deep desire for revenge hiding behind his words, nor of the impossibility of filling the great emptiness they masked. But on that night I understood that the war against the oligarchs was only a start. It wasn't just a question of regaining control of a few companies that had fallen into the wrong hands. We had to mobilize all of our resources, all the elements of Russia's power, to recover our place on the world stage. A sovereign democracy, that was our goal. And to bring it about, we needed men of steel, men who could perform the primordial function of any state: to be a weapon of defense and aggression. And these men were the *siloviki*, the men of the security services. Putin was one of their number. The most powerful, the most savvy. The toughest. But one of their own. He knew them, had confidence in them and no one else. He placed them in positions of power—in top government positions, of course, but also at the head of private companies, which he gradually took back from the hands of the opportunists of the 1990s. Energy, raw materials, transportation, communications. In every sector, the oligarchs were replaced by strongmen, the *siloviki*. That's how the state once again became the source of all things in Russia.

You're going to tell me that what resulted was a corrupt system? A system where the ministers are also CEOs, as those bloggers would so like to prove, sitting there in Moscow in their three-hundred-dollar jeans and taking us to task for our villas, our boats, our private jets? But isn't it also true that when Winston Churchill was the first lord of the admiralty, he had the use of the Royal Navy's yacht the *Enchantress*, where he would entertain his millionaire friends in return for their hospitality to him in Switzerland or on the Côte d'Azur? During the First World War, the Duke of Westminster would lend him his Rolls, and when he traveled to the United States, his industrialist friends would offer him their private railroad carriages. In California, he stayed at San Simeon, the home of William Randolph Hearst, or in a suite at the Biltmore, paid for by God knows who. Did any of this keep him from being one of the main figures of the twentieth century? Of course not, in fact just the opposite. Why should a statesman have to live like a postal employee?

This idea that men in the public sector have to live like poor stooges is profoundly immoral. The government needs to maintain its rank. Its servants can't be nobodies who haven't made it in the private sector, people who show up with their hands outstretched, asking for charity. Our great contribution has been to create a new elite that brings together a great deal of power with a great deal of money. Strongmen who can sit down at any table, unhampered by the complexes your ragged politicians and powerless businessmen suffer from. People who are whole, who can use the entire range of instruments that impact reality: power, money, even violence when necessary. Your pseudo-CEOs can't stand up to an elite like this, which seems to have sprung from an earlier age, from the era of the great patricians of ancient Rome, the time of the founders of world-spanning empires.

Power doesn't necessarily corrupt, it may also improve a man, as long as he can handle it. Every leader asks for loyalty above all, but many make the mistake of seeking it from weak or mediocre men. Terrible idea: they're always the first to betray. The weak can't afford the luxury of being sincere. Or loyal. The tsar knows that loyalty is a trait found in those capable of cultivating it—the strong, those who are sure enough of themselves to nurture it. That said, it's clear that the struggle for power in Russia, compared to other places, is savage and unorthodox. Anything can happen at any moment. The rules are ferocious, because the stakes themselves are.

19

I LANDED IN NICE on a fall morning. The air smelled of salt and pine resin. Two heavies in Prada were waiting on the runway to take me to the Château de la Garoupe. What they called a château was actually an unsightly villa built by an English baron at the turn of the twentieth century and afterwards degraded further by a series of subsequent owners. The area had originally been a paradise, but Antibes had gradually become a kind of three-star luxury resort, and though the villas on the peninsula might merit an added half star or so, they hadn't entirely been spared the general program of uglification to which Berezovsky had become a recent and enthusiastic convert.

Boris, lavish with his millions, had bought several neighboring houses and joined them into a single grandiose property. He greeted me in the forecourt, apparently in good spirits, dressed like a financier on vacation, in khaki pants and a striped shirt. He gave off a sense of overexcited melancholy. "This beach is where Picasso used to draw in the sand," he said, taking me on a tour of the property. "Cole Porter composed 'Love for Sale' in this room." As he spoke, the culture of the 1920s was transformed into selling points for a real estate transaction.

Once we'd settled in his second-floor office, I laid out the reason for my visit. Our intelligence services had reported a rumor—actually quite a bit more than a rumor—that Berezovsky was one of the main supporters of the Ukrainian opposition, which was beginning to give the tsar serious concerns. The idea that Russia was losing control of what had for centuries been an integral part of its territory was literally driving him mad. "Go see that son of a bitch," he'd told me, "tell him he's gone too far, and try to reason with him."

I was trying to do just that, but as usual, wasn't having much success. Boris's perorations had a circular quality, always returning more or less to their starting point.

"Do you know what the problem is, Vadya?"

—Of course I do, Boris, the problem is that Putin is a spy.

—No listen, Vadya, he's not a spy. Your boss worked in counterespionage. That's not the same at all! Do you know the difference? Spies look for accurate information, that's their job. But people in counterespionage, their job is to be paranoid. To see plots and traitors everywhere, and to invent them if necessary. That's their training. Paranoia is a professional duty. To the tsar's way of thinking, nothing ever happens spontaneously. There's always manipulation involved. With protests or the people's indignation, nothing is ever what it seems. There always has to be someone behind the scenes pulling the strings, a puppet master who's pursuing his own agenda. That's how your chief interpreted the submarine incident, when journalists were just doing their job and people had every reason to be angry. And that's what he thinks now about Ukraine. As if the poor Ukrainians didn't have their own valid reasons to rebel against the crooks who govern them.

—They certainly have good reasons, Boris, but they also have the thirty million dollars you sent them.

—So what? That's called politics, Vadya. And you know what else? It's called democracy. But you've already forgotten what that word means.

Beyond the windows, the worn landscape of the Riviera dulled the sharp edge of Berezovsky's words.

"Do you know," I said, "who the main supporters of the Ukrainian opposition are? Shall I list them for you? There's the CIA, the U.S. State Department, the big U.S. foundations, and George Soros's Open Society. And then there's you, the man who fought at our side to save Russia from disaster, who held that the Kremlin's authority had to be restored."

—And what of it? You're the ones who threw me out. I'm not here by choice, I might remind you. I live in exile, Vadya. Because if I ever set foot in Russia again, I'll wind up in jail like your friend Khodorkovsky. You people took everything I had, Vadya, so what am I supposed to do, say thank you?

I looked around at the mahogany tables, the Louis XV mantelpiece, the bronze candlesticks, the acanthus scrolls, the marble busts. All of it slightly wrong for this place, which, after all, was a glorified beach house, but Berezovsky had never quite grasped the concept of minimalism. He followed my gaze.

"All of it is mine, Vadya," he said. "Earned by the sweat of my brow. Even if you wanted, you couldn't do anything about it."

—Be fair, Boris. Up till now, the tsar has stayed friends with you, in spite of your disagreements. That's why you were able to sell the shares of your companies in Russia. How much did you get? Around one point three billion dollars, if I remember?

—A lot less than they were worth.

—But enough all the same to guarantee a life of comfort for you and your descendants, I should think.

—If I'd wanted a comfortable life, Vadya, I'd have stayed at the university and taught math.

For a moment, the ghost of Berezovsky as a graying professor in corduroys and a Shetland sweater hovered in the air between us.

"What I'm trying to tell you, Boris," I said patiently, "is that you'd be wise not to underestimate what you have. Anyone else would take full advantage of it."

—Or else what? You send your hired killers after me? Look around, Vadya, I've got my sidemen too. And mine are better than yours because I pay them ten times as much.

—Don't be vulgar, Boris. I didn't come here to threaten you. Just to appeal to your sense of patriotism. I understand your resentment, but I can't believe it's blinded you to the point of turning on your own country.

—Putin's Russia is not my country, Berezovsky shot back. I don't recognize it anymore. We had our faults, but for the first time in Russian history, we'd managed to build a free country, one where people could do and say what they wanted. For the first time in eleven centuries of history, Vadya, think of it. And in a few years, you ripped the whole thing up, everything. You turned Russia back into what it's always been: a gigantic prison.

—No one should feel too sorry for the Russians. They have one hundred and twenty television channels.

—But those channels all tell the same story, Vadya, like in Brezhnev's time.

I was about to answer when we were interrupted by a butler dressed in white. Lunch was served. We went downstairs to join a small group of people gathered in the drawing room.

"Dear friends," said Berezovsky, "allow me to introduce Vadim Baranov, the real brains of my friend Vladimir Putin, tsar of all the Russias."

A chance for hyperbole was something Boris could never pass up. The lunch guests turned to look at me with mild interest. Theirs were the tired eyes of people who habitually dine at places like the Château de la Garoupe. An elegant elderly lady. A real estate developer in his fifties who left the lower button on his jacket sleeve undone to show that it had been custom-tailored. Two decorative young ladies who spoke mostly to each other. And a competent-looking Nordic businessman who was visibly ill at ease with the Mediterranean ambience.

I was about to launch myself at the drinks tray, as being the sole antidote to the hours of deadly boredom ahead, when I suddenly felt a strong burst of energy, like a radioactive beam, emanating from the dining room. I turned to discover its source. Beyond the wide-open double glass doors stood a perfect creature, a lustrous presence. Lightly tanned, she wore a white tunic that came to just above her knees. Her gray shark eyes looked at me without a trace of emotion. It was Ksenia. She'd lost none of her splendor, which seemed in fact enhanced by the passage of time. A kind of warrior virtue seemed to inhabit her features, replacing the childish capriciousness I'd known. Ksenia in Berezovsky's dining room radiated the beauty of an army drawn up in battle formation. We nodded at each other, unsmiling. Everything, past as well as present, enjoined us to behave as enemies. Yet I detected no hostility on her part, nor did I feel any animosity toward her. It seemed instead as though I'd found a lost talisman, one that had been long forgotten but whose power the passage of time had left unaltered.

My main occupation during lunch was not to look at her. In the early going, the conversation was no help at all. The tanned quinquagenarian, who did in fact turn out to be a London mega-realtor, was comparing the services offered by the private aircraft terminals at Nice with those at Cannes. One of the young women was describing a contemporary art opening at a Monte Carlo gallery. Someone else was decrying the fact that the Hôtel du Cap now allowed the use of credit cards. My attention zeroed in on the small lobsters we'd been served, their shells already cracked to spare us the least inconvenience.

At a certain point, Berezovsky directed the conversation toward every Russian's favorite topic: Russia, Russians, and our characteristic idiosyncrasies and paradoxes. He spoke to his guests in the bantering tones he'd once used with his acquaintances at Logovaz House.

"We don't belong to the same race as the rest of you, I'll have you know. We have white skin, yes, and a few other things in common, but the difference in mentality between a Russian and a Westerner is as great as between an Earthling and a Martian. If I may, Baroness, I'd like to tell you a story about a character from early in the last century, probably an ancestor of our friend Vadya."

At that, the eyes of the lunch guests turned briefly toward me before reverting once more to our host.

"He belonged to the aristocracy, this Sergei, and when the October Revolution broke out he went north to fight the Bolsheviks. After the Red faction wiped out the last resistance, he fled into exile, first to Berlin, then to Paris, where he immediately became a pillar of the White Russian community. It included princes who drank with horse thieves, Cossacks who'd become nightclub bouncers—a fringe group, living above their means, believing that the Bolsheviks would eventually be thrown out and all the palaces and estates returned to their rightful owners. 'To next year in Saint Petersburg!' they chorused, their glasses raised, pretending not to know their time was past, once and for all."

A great sigh emanated from the baroness, who clearly belonged to that backstairs nobility in England whose members can, at reasonable rates, be rented to fill out a weekend gathering or a boardroom vacancy. Berezovsky sailed on.

"Sergei was always the first to call for a party and the last to leave the table—a quality, as you know, that Russians respect highly. After a time, however, his finances began to show the strain, and he had almost nothing left. Until one night, a friend took him aside and said: 'With the money you have left, Seryoga, there's just enough to buy yourself a taxi license. Think about your future, or you'll end up living under a bridge.' What would any of you have done, you West-erners of good sense and extensive education?"

Boris reined himself in and glared at his guests around the lunch table.

"I'll tell you what you would have done, you'd have quietly taken off your riding boots, pulled your taxi driver's beret low over your forehead, and re-signed yourself to a lifetime of making runs between the Étoile and the Gare de Lyon, which was the only logical course. But what did Sergei do? He thought for a long moment. He gave his friend's shoulder a squeeze. He got to his feet, walked over to the maître d'hôtel, and in the voice he'd used to sound his regi-ment's last charge at Arkhangelsk, called out: 'Cham-pagne all around!' That, don't you see, is a Russian. A Russian is somebody who buys everyone a last round of champagne with his taxi license money!"

The baroness trilled appreciatively. It was the least she could do, as the master of the house had seemingly told the story for her benefit. For my part, I doubted its authenticity; I seemed to remember that Joseph Kessel had told a similar anecdote in one of his early short stories. I also had the suspicion that Berezovsky had dug it up on my behalf. I am a real Russian, he was telling me, and I'll never trade in my crazy ways for a taxi license.

"I don't think it's anything to brag about, Boris," said Ksenia, speaking up for the first time. "Look at them all, racing through the streets of Moscow in their

Mercedes, with their SUV escorts, their rotary lights, and their cell phone scramblers. Doesn't it look as if they're playacting? Auditioning for a part in the Russian *Mission: Impossible*?"

—Everyone is always playacting, I'm sorry to say.

—But only the Russians do it so badly, she retorted.

—I don't know how things work in Russia, said the developer, who'd decided to thrust himself into the conversation, but in Africa, to take an example, there can also be a practical aspect. The policeman knows that if you have the money to buy a big car, you also have the money to buy his boss. So he stays away from Mercedes 600s.

Ksenia looked at him as if he were a speck of mud that had dropped from her shoe. "That didn't work so well in our case. We had a fleet of Mercedes, but the cops came for us anyway."

Silence, smiles of embarrassment. This time, people carefully avoided looking at me. I knew from experience that the important thing when you're attacked in conversation is not to alter your position, to remain impassive while preparing a counterattack. Without batting an eyelid, I opted for a diversionary tactic.

"There, Boris, you see? Contrary to what you think, Russia is not a banana republic!"

It was a monstrous lie, of course. But who has the courage to call out a lie when it issues from the mouth of power? Especially at a social gathering around a lunch table. Even the master of the house offered no reply. It would have been a sign of weakness, and Berezovsky had learned over the years that any sign of weakness can cost you. After a brief hesitation, the conversation set off again along smoother paths. For a moment, I thought I saw a distant flame shoot up in Ksenia's eyes, then just as suddenly go out.

2 0

A FEW DAYS AFTER my trip to the Côte d'Azur, the situation in Ukraine degenerated. Rebels, supported by the Americans, refused to accept the election results. They occupied the main square in Kiev, where they sang, waved their orange ribbons, and chanted pro-Western slogans. Suddenly, international watchdog commissions, delegations of U.S. congresspeople, and European Union diplomatic missions showed up out of nowhere, all of them agreeing that the pro-Russian candidate's election victory was fraudulent. Elections had just been held in Afghanistan and Iraq, with bombs exploding in the streets and polling places full of American soldiers—but no problem there, clearly everything was aboveboard. Not so in Ukraine, of course. There would have to be a revote, because the result came out wrong. So the Ukrainian government was forced to hold a second election, and this time the pro-American candidate won, the guy who wanted to make Ukraine a NATO member. Ukraine—the birthplace of Khrushchev and Brezhnev, the headquarters of our naval fleet—a part of NATO!

They'd called it the "Orange Revolution." Precisely, a revolution! It was the final assault on what remained of Russian power. The year before, it had happened in Georgia. There, they'd called it the "Rose Revolution"! In that case, too, the upshot of the revolution, with its pretty girls and noble ideals, had been the installation of a CIA spy to head the government. You didn't need a crystal ball to imagine where they were headed next: Russia. A big color-coded revolution in Moscow, a new president with maybe a master's from Yale on his résumé, and the United States' victory would be complete. Bush Junior could star in another of those masquerades he liked so much. "Mission accomplished!"—but this time coming to you directly from Red Square.

The strongmen all went to work immediately. Their tactic was to put the usual countermeasures in place—expel the Western infiltrators, neutralize the agitators, get tighter control of the media. These were certainly all useful measures, but I personally doubted how effective they would be. In cases of this kind, the use of force is always proof of negligence, stemming from a lack of imagination, and it rarely resolves problems in a lasting way.

My own approach was different. I remembered a strange character I'd met once or twice back when I was regularly seeing Limonov. A colossus of a man, well over six feet in height, always dressed in black leather, with an abundant mane of jet-black hair down to his shoulders, he was known as Alexander Zaldostanov. To all appearances, he was just another biker in the vast gallery of eccentric characters that Eduard liked having around him. He'd caught my attention because once, when we were dining with Limonov and his "people's commissaries," while his colleagues stuffed their faces with fried haunches of pork, Zaldostanov was picking at a plate of steamed shrimp with a green bean and pomegranate salad. "My parents were physicians in Kirovograd," he'd explained, "and I have a medical degree from the Third Moscow Medical Institute. I used to be a plastic surgeon."

At a certain point, he had realized it was more fun to break jaws than to reconstruct them. But he'd kept a sharpness and a delicacy about him that most of his companions lacked. In the late 1980s, he'd founded one of the first biker clubs in the Soviet Union, modeling it on the Hells Angels. The Night Wolves had started out as centaurs, prowling the streets on their old Soviet-era bikes, looking for fights, breaking shop windows, and evading the police—typical, slightly naive rebels of the kind living in our exurbs at that time. After the Soviet Union collapsed, they'd made a qualitative leap and become a criminal gang that lived off racketeering and trafficking of every kind. "It felt like living in a science fiction movie," Zaldostanov once told me.

"Civilization had crumbled away, and we'd inherited the world. Or what was left of it." The gang included Slavs, Chechens, Uzbeks, Dagestanis, Siberians—all sharing a passion for high-displacement engines and a taste for adventure. Almost all of them had huge tattoos. Imperial eagles, icons of Christ in Majesty, portraits of Stalin. Coherence didn't count for much, what mattered was that all these images were symbols of Russian greatness. That's what had drawn them together around Limonov.

Eduard was an intellectual, not stupid at all, and so by definition useless. But that wasn't the case with Alexander. Zaldostanov was a real patriot, a man of action and a gang leader. Maybe the moment had come to let his rage have full vent. And the rage of all the good old boys around him—not one of whom, if I remember, weighed less than 235 pounds.

I'd arranged to meet him at the office. Zaldostanov showed up in his leather jacket, with a three-day beard, and a faint I-don't-give-a-damn expression. But he was an intelligent man, he wasn't indifferent to the setting in which he found himself. Not only had he never set foot inside the Kremlin, the idea that he might do so one day had never crossed his mind. From the way he moved, the furtive glances he darted around him, I gathered that the biker considered this summons a somewhat miraculous event.

Several times I've noticed that the fiercest rebels are among those most affected by the pomp and circumstance of power. And the more they piss and moan at the gates, the more they yelp with joy once through the door. Unlike eminent men, who often hide anarchic impulses behind their easy familiarity with gilded rooms, rebels are invariably dazzled, like wild animals caught in the headlights.

Zaldostanov made a show of keeping his composure, but I felt I could read his mind. We spent the first minutes talking about the heroic days of the National Bolshevik Party, avoiding any mention of Eduard, who had just finished his first two-year jail sentence. But there was no time to waste, and I decided to give him the coup de grâce.

"The president has been informed of our meeting and sends you his greetings," I said.

At this news, the biker's three-hundred-plus pounds seemed to levitate for a moment above his chair. Zaldostanov was living one of his life's high points.

"I've been following your activities these last few years, and I have to tell you that I'm very impressed, Alexander. You're phenomenal. You take these youths and you give them a home, a discipline. You turn these strays, these lost souls, into soldiers capable of accomplishing extraordinary things. I see that you've set up a real business, with the bar, the concerts, and even merchandizing!"

—When they come to us, they find the two things they're looking for: brotherhood and strength, said Zaldostanov gravely.

—Exactly, I said, brotherhood and strength. And if I read this right, you're not just a biker gang. You're really a group of true Russian patriots.

Zaldostanov assented: "Faith and the fatherland, Vadim Alexeievich. We turn from Satan and go toward God, against the current. We're ready to knock heads, but not for a kilo of cocaine. We have other values."

—Quite so, Alexander. Wolves aren't just predators, they're also guardians of the forest.

The biker looked at me, mildly perplexed. Was I laying it on too thick? I decided to get down to business. "Have you seen," I asked, "what's happening in Ukraine?"

—Sure, they're having a revolution.

"That's not quite accurate, Alexander. A revolution comes from below, it gives power to the people. What happened in Ukraine was a coup d'état. And who do you think came into power?" Zaldostanov was listening to me with an air of intense concentration, but said nothing. "The Americans, Alexander. The Orange Revolution didn't start on Maidan Square, it started in Langley, Virginia. But you have to give it to them, the CIA did its work well, not like in the past. In the old days, they would pay off the generals. And if you triggered a military coup at the right moment, the thing was in the bag. They did that for years, and it worked very well. But nowadays it's more complicated. There's the internet, cell phones, cameras. So, guess what? They changed their playbook. In fact, they turned it on its head: instead of starting at the top, they started at the bottom. It was a case of power embracing antipower. They studied their enemies' techniques. Guerrillas, pacifists, the youth movement. And they understood how it worked."

Or at least that was the tsar's deeply held conviction.

"Look at Ukraine, Alexander. They created a young people's organization, they held concerts on Maidan Square, they set up an NGO to monitor elections, so-called, and media that they claimed was independent, though it was controlled, as it happens, by the most anti-Russian oligarchs in existence. Even the orange ribbon. I'll bet they had a poll to choose the color. Everything is calculated, just like when they launch a new detergent. Or better, a new drink for teenagers. Because the main ingredient is energy, the frustration of the young, their desire to change the world. The Americans understand this, and they're making the most of it.

"Basically, Eduard was right. There's an existential question underlying everything, the question that torments every young person. What should I do with my life? How can I make a difference? It's not a political question. But there are times in history when, if a system can't return a satisfactory answer, it will get swept away. It's perfectly normal for the most enterprising young people to want to do things, to look for a cause. And for an enemy. What we have to do is give them that cause and that enemy—before they choose one themselves.

"But unfortunately we're not in a position to do that. Look around you, Alexander. Nothing here but bureaucrats in suit and tie, politicians, party representatives. We represent the power structure, we're like the guy in that movie Eduard is always talking about, the one who says 'Plastics!' to the college grad who asks him what he should do with his life. We're the grown-ups, the enemy."

—Whereas I'm...

—You're an adult too, Alexander. But you've taken a different path in life. You haven't made any compromises. You represent freedom, adventure. Your vital energy is still intact. A person only has to look at you to know it. Young people sense that straight off. And you understand them. You know what they want. You know how to talk to them and what to say. You can guide them so they don't fall into the trap the Americans have set for them. You can lead them toward real values. The fatherland. Faith.

—Possibly, but working all alone, you know...

—You won't be alone, Alexander. The tsar will be behind you, and he'll protect you. He's not like us, here in the Kremlin. He's not a bureaucrat, a suit. The tsar is like you. He belongs to the order of conquerors. He was made to be your leader, the leader of all the true patriots in this land. Didn't he set Russia back on its feet? And why do you think the Americans want to get rid of him? Because they find Russia bearable only when the country is on its knees, they can't accept anyone challenging their supremacy. And also, he's just like you. Physical exercise is his religion, competing. He practices judo, he hunts, he loves driving at high speed...

—Do you think he'd come to one of our meets?

—Of course, he's dying to! And it won't take much persuading once he learns that you're all on his side, that you want to help him fight for Russia's greatness. Our country has always successfully fended off attacks, from Napoleon, from Hitler. Now it's our turn to do our duty.

Zaldostanov had by this point stopped listening to me. Already, he saw himself astride his bike, hair flying, shoulder to shoulder with the tsar, a kind of post-atomic Cossack.

"But we'll do more than that," I said. "We'll organize the Russian version of Maidan Square, a gathering for all the young patriots in the country, a place where they can see each other face-to-face. And we'll take the battle to our real enemy, Western decadence and its false values, with all the divisiveness and frustration that it's brought!"

—Right, the Russian Maidan Square, that's huge...

Zaldostanov was starting to get excited. It was slowly dawning on him that my plan would allow him to reconcile the dreams of glory he'd had as a twenty-year-old with the legitimate pecuniary ambitions of the fortysomething he'd become.

"We'll organize other gatherings, too, and concerts, summer camps," I said. "Then we'll need schools for special training, newspapers, internet sites—everything that goes into making a new generation of patriots. We've got to lead an attack on the mediocrity of everyday life, Alexander! Offer our youngsters a real alternative to Western materialism. Russia has to become a place where you can vent your anger against the world and still be a faithful servant of the tsar. The two things aren't contradictory, quite the opposite."

—In practical terms, said Zaldostanov, what you want to do is make revolution impossible.

Though carried away with enthusiasm, the biker had lost none of the solid good sense I'd detected in him from the start.

"Let's just say we want to remove the need for it," I said. "Why start a revolution if the system already incorporates it?"

21

ALTHOUGH I DIDN'T SERVE him a drop of vodka, Zaldostanov left the Kremlin that day in an intoxicated state. What he didn't know was that after seeing him, I had a meeting with the leader of a group of young Communists, who'd impressed me with their vivacity. Then I met with the intriguing spokesperson for an Orthodox revival movement. After her, I met with the head of Spartak's ultras. Then with a representative of one of the most popular bands in the alternative music scene. Bit by bit, I recruited them all—the bikers and the hooligans, the anarchists and the skinheads, the Communists and the religious fanatics, the Far Right, the Far Left, and most of those in the middle. Anyone likely to respond in an exciting way to the demand of Russian youths for meaning. After what had happened in Ukraine, we couldn't allow the forces of anger to go unsupervised. If we were going to construct a truly strong system, it wasn't enough to have a monopoly on power, we would also need a monopoly on subversion. Once again, it came down to using reality as the raw material for creating a kind of higher-order game. I'd done nothing all my life but probe the elasticity of the world, its inexhaustible propensity for paradox and contradiction. The political theater now taking shape under my direction was the natural outcome of a long trajectory.

I have to say that everyone played the part I'd assigned them willingly. Some even showed talent. The only factions I didn't approach were the university professors, the technocrats who'd been responsible for the disasters of the 1990s, the flag bearers of political correctness, and the progressives battling for transgender bathrooms. I decided to let the opposition have them. And this was precisely the constituency that we wanted the opposition to have. In a sense, they became my best actors, working for us without ever needing to be recruited. Many were inbred Muscovites, the kind who feel they're on foreign soil the moment they venture beyond the outer ring road, people who would be incapable of moving an armchair—let alone governing Russia...Every time they opened their mouths, they added to our popularity and put it on a firmer footing. The economists parading their PhDs, the oligarchs who'd survived the 1990s, the human rights professionals, the feminists, the ecologists, the vegans, the gay rights activists—they were manna from heaven as far as we were concerned. When that girl band desecrated the Cathedral of Christ the Savior, yelling obscenities at Putin and the Russian patriarch, we got a five-point boost in the polls.

Then there was Garry Kasparov, the chess champion who founded his own opposition party. I met him only once, at one of those social events in Moscow that seem to gather everything and its opposite. It wasn't a setting I normally frequented, but you can't imagine how hard it is to escape the solicitations of a determined hostess. Anastasia Chekhova had ruled over Moscow society for years, combining the cultural aura that came from being the descendant of a great writer with the buying power that came from her banker husband. She lived in a small townhouse that had been built in the early twentieth century by a grain merchant who had managed to enjoy it only briefly.

The entrance hall, lined with turquoise fabric, led to two large mahogany doors with copper handles, sculpted to resemble birds. These opened onto a succession of drawing rooms decorated in the Jazz Age style, their console tables, sofas, and coffee tables forming an intricate geometry that effectively framed Chekhova's stunning collection of ancient jades. Amid the polished surfaces of the furniture and the mirrors reflecting flowers, one almost expected to bump into Zelda Fitzgerald, or at least Kiki de Montparnasse. Most of the time, though, you would end up talking to a trendy hairdresser or, at best, a correspondent for the *New York Times*.

These soirees were too choreographed to be much fun, but people attended them all the same for the confirmation it gave to their sense of social importance. In the absence of true gaiety, the guests' eyes shone with a rapacious desire to get information ahead of anyone else, thus gaining entrance to a dimension where everything happened a little early. This slight advance on the rest of the world could, with a modicum of skill, be converted into precious goods: money, power, prestige.

The mistress of the house planned her receptions like military campaigns. Imperious, she swept through Moscow's social elite like an icy, variable wind. And while her goal was always social success, she achieved her strategy by mobilizing a variety of different resources. Businessmen provided the foundation and substance of a Chekhova gathering and aristocrats its embellishment. But for the party to be a true success, some rarer ingredients had to be added—a dollop of genius, a pinch of international glamour, and a hint of transgression. Garry Kasparov had the advantage of combining all three attributes in one person. A chess player with a worldwide reputation, he had entered politics by organizing so-called dissident marches in the streets of the capital, immediately lending him a halo of drawing room heroism. The jewel-covered matrons belonging to Moscow's radical chic clamored around him as if he were the new Che Guevara.

On my arrival that particular night, I found him surrounded by a rapt audience and clearly drunk on his own social glory, and perhaps something else as well. At a certain point, someone must have pointed out to him that I was there.

"Ah, Baranov," he said, "there you are, the Wizard of the Kremlin, Putin's Rasputin. Do you know what people are saying about your 'sovereign democracy'? That it is to democracy what an electric chair is to a chair."

I burst out laughing. "Well, at least it shows that Russians haven't lost their sense of humor! But seriously, Kasparov, do you know what's meant by sovereign democracy?"

—I'm no political theorist, he said, but speaking as a chess player, I'd say that it's the opposite of a chess match. In chess, the rules are constant, but the winner always changes. In your sovereign democracy, the rules change, but the winner is always the same.

The champion had game, no doubt about it. The socialites around us twitched like groupies at a concert.

"Possibly," I said. "I know politics is not your area of expertise, but tell me, Kasparov, didn't the Christian Democratic Union stay in power in Germany for twenty years after World War II? And the Liberal Democratic Party in Japan for forty years? You liberals think that our political culture in Russia is archaic and a product of ignorance. You think our Russian habits and traditions are an obstacle to progress. You want to ape Westerners, but you're missing the main thing."

Kasparov was by this time looking at me with a frankly hostile gaze.

"If you want to taste something sweet," I went on, "you have to eat the candy, not the wrapper. To win freedom, you have to grasp its substance, not its outward form. You repeat slogans you've learned in Washington or Berlin, and in the meantime fill our streets with candy wrappers. You're like the Bourbon dynasty, never forgetting anything and never learning anything—you had your chance, and you left Russia in shreds. Ever since being removed from power, you've dreamed of coming back to finish what you started. On our side, we've looked into the question thoroughly. We've learned what the West has to teach and adapted it to the reality of Russia. Sovereign democracy corresponds to the deepest foundations of Russian political culture. That's why the people are on our side. You professors are the only ones who haven't understood this."

—But I'm not a professor!

—Of course not. You're a chess champion.

Kasparov grasped the irony, which he didn't appreciate. A true son of the Caucasus, he pursed his lips in a sign of menace.

"You won't find a game," he said, "more violent than chess."

I gave him a soft smile.

"You don't have a clue what you're talking about, professor. Politics is infinitely more violent."

—But politics is not a game, he said.

—Not for amateurs, it's not a game. But for professionals, believe me, it's the only game worth playing.

Kasparov looked at me as if I were a madman. At the same time, I thought I saw him repress a shiver.

22

I'VE ALWAYS LIKED THE bars of grand hotels. At any pretentious restaurant, you have to reserve ahead of time and are exposed to the buffooneries of the latest star chef; by contrast, every hotel bar, even the most legendary, stands ready and waiting, its doors open to a variegated clientele that might include tourists in a happy frame of mind, businessmen of greater or lesser shadiness, and women of uncertain status. The air you breathe in these places is generally neutral, and nothing so much resembles the bar of a grand hotel in London as the bar of a grand hotel in Lisbon, Singapore, or Moscow. Same soft lighting, opaque mirrors, fake wood paneling. Same music, same servers, same menu. Their strength lies in offering the right mix of comfort and indifference. Whatever city in the world you find yourself in, without a guide, you only have to make your way at some point in the evening to the bar of a grand hotel. That's all you need for a sense of well-being—as long as you strictly avoid the trendy places, the boutique hotels, and other such traps.

In Moscow at that time, hotel bars were my oases. For a few hours I could pretend to look at the brutal reality I was immersed in from the outside, adopting the perspective of the tourist or the visiting businessman. Just seeing the fauna, sprawled on the sofas with their slightly relieved expressions, gave me a sense of calm. Somewhat as if the revolving doors in the lobby had the power to keep the city's dark matter from coming inside, creating a little custom-built Switzerland.

At the Metropol, it generally took only a sip or two of whiskey before I felt transported to the prosperous and innocuous shores of Lake Geneva. But on this particular night, uncharacteristically, I was totally focused on the present. Sitting across from me was Ksenia, who had ordered a glass of sparkling water. I'd managed, through persistence, to get her to agree to a meeting, but this hardly meant that she was in any way ready to gratify me. She had honed to a fine edge the feminine art of saying no while signaling yes with her head, of smiling while delivering an insult, and of offering and withholding herself at the same time without ever falling into contradiction. In her presence, a man could feel both a sense of victory and an awareness of the impossibility of victory. Also the extent to which the two are inextricably bound. And the extent to which they form the basis of desire, perhaps even of love.

I had a confused awareness of all this at the time. I was still searching for something, but it was only later that I would realize what it was. On this first evening, I tried to learn what she had been doing during the past few years. Nothing, she said. It was true. Now I remembered it. Ksenia didn't believe in work. Or in making any effort on behalf of anything but herself. While the wives and partners of oligarchs started contemporary art galleries or foundations for rescuing Russian orphans or Arctic seals, Ksenia did nothing. Her laziness, intact from compromise, was a form of wisdom. She felt no need to append an activity of any sort to her existence, which automatically made her superior to everyone else. Her strength lay not just in the beauty with which she took possession of any space but also in the incredible quality of her gestures. Ksenia was, all on her own, a doctrine. Not the abstract matter that appears on university exams, but true philosophy, a question of life and death, which alone is worth engaging. There was something in her that aroused in men an irresistible nostalgia for the lives they'd failed to live. And the desire to tell her about them. Tell her anything so as not to lose her attention. Her presence opened the possibility of miracles. Or at any rate gave that impression.

I spoke to her as I had not spoken in years. As I'd perhaps never spoken to anyone, and with the sense that I would be understood. It's perfectly possible that this was simply a technique that Ksenia had developed, an optical effect she managed to produce, the reflection of a mirage and nothing more. But it was enough for me. I told her how, a few days earlier, I'd run to catch an elevator in the Kremlin and suddenly seen my face in the mirror. Only it wasn't me staring back from the elevator wall, it was my father. He'd appeared unexpectedly, but he now dogged my steps. I saw him every morning while shaving; he looked at me with surprise and a touch of irony. My father's face, which I'd come to inhabit despite my many efforts to avoid it. And the skull behind it, now clearly coming into view, awaiting its hour, etching its imprint on my features, as they became ever more drawn. I told her about my tiredness. And for the first time, as I spoke to Ksenia, I felt how truly tired I was. I'd run so much and for so long that, at the age of forty, I felt like an Olympic athlete ripe for retirement.

After our first get-together, we started to meet regularly at the Metropol. To all appearances, Ksenia was allowing herself to be guided, progressing from the glass of water at our first meeting to a glass of Chablis at our second, and subsequently graduating to a vodka martini. In reality, sitting across from me, her legs crossed, her small breasts pointing, she was gradually reasserting her reign. Her eyes smiled, then turned serious. Not for a moment in the years we had been separated had her intelligence stopped developing. She had drawn sustenance from everything and now came toward me pure and renewed. Ksenia exuded a sense of calm I'd never known her to have previously, as though her inner agitation had finally found its antidote in the chaotic events that marked her recent years. Her old suspicions about life and people had been confirmed, but so, too, had her capacity to understand and manage them. Talking to her was like ending an exile that had gone on for too long. Our thoughts chased each other and played like children on a sunny afternoon. Until the day when, out of carelessness, we ventured onto terrain that we had till then avoided.

The evening was already far along when, fueled by alcohol, I launched into the story of a Spanish Jesuit from the murky past who'd written a handbook to help vigorous, steadfast souls find their bearings. His thesis was that even if gallantry, generosity, and fidelity vanished from the earth, they could still be found in the heart of a man of valor.

Ksenia made a face.

"Glory, passion, you men are always such romantics. We women can't afford it, we're responsible for the world's survival."

It was now my turn to smile. I've always enjoyed having my most deeply rooted prejudices confirmed. One of the main aspects of a Russian woman's charm is her ferocity. And of the many Russian women I'd had occasion to meet, Ksenia was undoubtedly the fiercest. Her eyes drilled through me.

"Don't tell me that you're like all the others, Vadya. One of those men who'll never understand anything."

No, no, I never would understand, that must be entirely obvious. Far be it from me to claim the contrary. But Ksenia went on.

"You make big speeches, but afterwards you mix everything up. You basically think that marriage is a way of guaranteeing yourself an audience, of having someone always at your side to admire your exploits."

I wasn't sure she was addressing me.

"Not you, Vadya, you're a poet. A poet erring among wolves. Love is sacred to you, clearly, that I remember. 'Look, behind the forest where we walk in fear, As if it were a lighted castle, evening draws near.'"

—How lovely. Rilke, I'd forgotten him.

—Yes, how lovely! If it had been up to you, we'd still be sitting on the couch in Gasheka Street, holding hands.

—From what I remember, we didn't just hold hands on that couch.

For a moment, Ksenia's expression softened, but she quickly regrouped.

—Marriage is the opposite of love, you know. It's like taxes. In a way, it's something that you do for others.

—Right, I said, to build the future of socialism!

I couldn't understand why she had to give me this speech. Or maybe I did. In any case, I didn't want to hear it. But no one has ever stopped Ksenia once she's made up her mind to demonstrate something.

"Marriage is a law," she said, "the basis of any and all society. Isn't that what your tsar is always saying when he's with your Orthodox friends? That's why it's so ridiculous to imagine basing marriage on a passing feeling."

—But we can still raise a toast to passing feelings, no?

Impassive on her black velvet sofa, Ksenia ignored my raised glass.

"All over the world, for centuries, men and women married for reasons that had nothing to do with love, and they didn't go into it with foolish hopes—thinking, for instance, that a contract could lead them to happiness. In marriage, they found the stability they needed to start a family. And for everything else, they made do, and there are a thousand ways...Do you know that in eighteenth-century France, a husband and a wife were never invited to dinner together?"

—I love the fact that you've held on to some of the values of our old crowd.

The truth was that I didn't love it at all. I only wanted Ksenia to get off the subject, but there was nothing to be done.

"Do you know what's strange?" she said. "Once in a while the husband and wife would fall in love with each other. It was considered slightly embarrassing at the time, but it happened..."

—No, really!

—It has to be said that it usually didn't happen. But the marriage worked because its foundations were solid. And love was something you found elsewhere.

—The husband did, at any rate...

—The wife too, at least in the more evolved societies. You remember how it used to work here in the Soviet era? The husbands and wives went off on vacation at different times. It was done on purpose, there were different vacation spots for each. So they both would have a chance to make the most of it... The crackpot notion of marrying for love comes from nineteenth-century novels, from Hollywood movies. Except that you learn after the fact that love doesn't last, or that it never existed, or that there's a greater love the next block over.

Ksenia's spontaneous cynicism had always fascinated me. But in this case, it didn't add up.

"When you left me," I said, "you no longer loved me."

—And how could I, Vadya? You were a spoiled young man, playing at being an artist, hiding out. You know my background, Vadya, I'd already done bohemia. It wasn't what I wanted. It doesn't provide you with freedom, you're always on the run. My mother thought of herself as a rebel, she wanted to be free, but as she got older she found herself becoming dependent on a man who agreed to look after her. That's when I understood that true freedom is a product of conformity. Only by keeping up appearances can you do what you want. I needed stability. Financial, yes. But other kinds too. Misha had control.

—Yes, right up until he lost it.

—That's because we live in a crazy country.

—Maybe. But in a normal country, Misha would at best have become an illegal bookmaker.

—I disagree. Misha would have been successful anywhere. But here he had to play by Russian rules.

—Only he never understood the rules here. If you buy something for four cents, and you've borrowed the money for it anyway, the thing doesn't belong to you, so it can be taken away at any time. Your Misha thought he was Steve Jobs.

—No, really, you're still mad at him, after all the damage your people did to him? You don't think he's paid enough already?

—No.

Ksenia looked at me oddly. For a moment I thought she was going to leave. Then her face assumed that look of frightening sweetness that was hers alone. Her eyes shone as brightly as a four-year-old's.

"You wanted me that much?"

—I loved you, Ksenia.

—And now? At this moment?

Silence.

"Still now."

At present, Ksenia was no longer a child. She was a woman at the height of her powers, and she smiled at me with the deep, sure smile of her forty years on earth. The strange and cruel nymph I had once known had grown up without losing any of her charm. I looked around me. The pianist had stopped playing. The tourists had gone off to bed. There were two waiters left, looking worried. Sitting across from each other, Ksenia and I found ourselves witnesses to something incomprehensible, like soldiers in a trench for the first time, suddenly living through what nothing could ever have prepared them for. Something that had started years earlier was coming to be, in a totally calm and unexpected way. Used as I was to the kind of event that leads off newscasts and makes people talk in the streets, I found myself completely unprepared for it. The imperceptible event that changes everything.

I remembered then how useless words are. A moment before, there had been no need for it, the moment after, nothing could have stopped it from happening. We left the hotel and started walking. All of Moscow's nighttime charm hovered around us. Overhead, the sky was deep and pure. We pushed into the narrow streets that ring the neighborhood around Tverskaya. Our footsteps sank into the snow, taking the place of words. The facades of the classic old houses and the branches of small trees covered in thick flakes escorted us in silence. Their benevolence removed all need of caution. We looked at each other from time to time, seeking confirmation in each other's eyes.

23

USING THE LABRADOR WAS not my idea. But you have to admit it was brilliant—if a little brutal, like most of the tsar's stratagems. The chancellor had prepared for a normal meeting. She turned up impeccably dressed, in a black pantsuit and ankle boots purchased at a discount store, as usual, and carrying no papers. Because she always studied up ahead of time: the meticulous files that her team produced, the notes with headings from the different ministries, and the memos on plain paper generated by the Federal Republic's security services. She spent whole days and nights absorbing data and gaming out geopolitical scenarios, with the same precision she'd used in carrying out laboratory experiments in her days as a university researcher. Consequently, the chancellor always arrived at meetings fresh and self-assured, ready to boss everyone around because she knew she could afford to, with the geometric power of the accumulated *Länder* and *Konzerne* behind her. That day, however, nothing could have prepared her for what she'd find on entering the meeting room. Koni. The tsar's huge Labrador retriever.

To fully grasp the situation, you have to know that the chancellor had a phobia for dogs. Over the years, she'd subdued more wild animals in the arena of world politics than all the lion tamers of the circus together. But a dog, any dog, even a tiny one, rekindled the primordial fear she'd felt at the age of eight when a neighbor's rottweiler had almost torn her to pieces under the horrified eyes of her father. Only a miracle saved her.

So imagine the scene in the Kremlin that day. Actually, you don't even need to imagine it, because the photos are found online. The chancellor smiling glassily while Koni stalks around her, his coat brushed to a high gloss. The chancellor petrified in her chair while Koni approaches playfully, looking to be petted. The chancellor on the verge of a nervous breakdown when Koni thrusts his snout into her lap, eager for a sniff of his new friend. The tsar, sitting next to her, is smiling and relaxed, his legs spread wide: "Are you sure the dog isn't bothering you, Chancellor Merkel? I could put her outside, but she's such a good dog. I hate to be separated from her."

The Labrador. That's the moment when the tsar decided to take his gloves off and start playing the game the way he'd learned it in a Leningrad schoolyard, where you'd barely get your foot on the ball before someone would already have kneed you in the groin. You always had to show that you were a little crazier than the rest if you didn't want the bullies to take it out on you. High-level politics is somewhat the same. Gilded drawing rooms, honor guards, official escorts through streets closed to traffic, but afterwards the same logic basically applies as in the schoolyard, where the bullies lay down the law, and the only way to get respect is to use your knee.

In the first years after he arrived on the international scene, the tsar had stayed on the fringes a bit, with the classic attitude of the Russian, whose papers are never fully in order and who has to submit to the detailed scrutiny of judges from more civilized parts. It's the age-old complex of the savage from the borderlands who has to atone for five centuries of rape and pillage, culminating in the apocalypse of real-world socialism. At the time, Moscow was full of skinny foreign experts. They swept through the big corporations, the ministries, and even the Kremlin with the air of Roman proconsuls sent to a distant outpost of empire to reestablish order. They took charge of banks, foundations, and newspapers, dispensing their advice and summary decisions in the tones of someone talking to a child he already knows will come to a bad end, despite all its parents' hard work.

We were used to listening to them. Because it was the only thing you could do, *There is no alternative.* But even though we did what they told us, things didn't improve. And somehow our influence keep decreasing. The more we tried to gain their acceptance, the less they seemed to take us into consideration. Then even that wasn't enough. Our docility called for the harshest punishment. NATO flooded into the Baltic States, and American military bases into central Asia. The oversight of financial institutions no longer sufficed; now they wanted to take power directly. Send us back to the basement and replace us with agents from the CIA and the International Monetary Fund. First in Georgia, then in Ukraine, the very heart of our lost empire.

On seeing furious mobs occupy Tbilisi, Kiev, and Bishkek and violently annul the results of their elections—with financing from George Soros, the U.S. Congress, and the European Union—the tsar finally understood. He was the real target. If he allowed the subversion of the color revolutions to go unchallenged, the contagion would spread to Russia and push him out of power, installing a Western puppet in his place. All the willingness he'd shown at the feet of the victors of the Cold War, sitting like a Russian schoolboy learning his manners, had been for nothing. It only convinced the new bosses there was no need for scruples. The road to Moscow was open. Total victory, which neither Napoleon nor Hitler had achieved, was finally within grasp.

That's when the tsar decided to bring out his Labrador. The tactic was not entirely original, as the precedent had already been set by a Roman emperor. But we Russians did him one better, because Caligula only made his horse a consul, whereas we promoted the dog to minister of foreign affairs.

Since then, the situation has improved markedly. Our partners have started to think of us in a different way, and step-by-step we regained the respect we'd lost on the international scene. Under Koni's leadership, Russia has reclaimed the rank of a major world power. Our voice has started to be heard again, both in Europe and the Middle East.

Of course, the Labrador's talents are unusual. First of all, it's a female, which automatically places her above her male colleagues. Next, she's a straight-line descendant of Brezhnev's favorite dog and is said to be named for Condoleezza Rice, the former U.S. secretary of state. So politics runs in her veins. But her most decisive quality is surprise. While her human colleagues are working out cautious strategies, consulting endless analyses, going back and forth, and not coming to any conclusion, Koni takes a quick sniff and goes into action. She is sovereign, she needs no one's permission to act. Under her leadership, we've learned to accept chaos, make it our ally. Don't go imagining any sweeping strategies. People think that the center of power operates with Machiavellian logic, when in fact it's a cauldron of passions and irrationality, a schoolyard, as I say, where random nastiness runs rampant and invariably triumphs over justice, and even over pure and simple logic. Of all the primates, man has the biggest brain, true, but also the biggest cock, bigger even than the gorilla's. Surely that must mean something, no?

The old Soviet leaders had their good qualities, but they invariably opted for stability over uncertainty. They wanted things to be organized, predictable. And in the end, that's why the Americans beat them. Because you Westerners are better at that game. Your whole vision of the world is based on avoiding accidents. On reducing the domain of uncertainty as much as possible so that reason can reign supreme. We, on the other hand, have understood that chaos is our friend, that it's in fact our only chance. Comparing the mercenaries and hackers that Koni has put in play with the functionaries of the earlier KGB, as your analysts do, is laughable. The former were predictable bureaucrats, whereas with the current crew we don't even know exactly what they will do tomorrow. But we've placed our bets on them. It was enough for the Labrador to show them the way, and they took off. That's all they were waiting for.

24

I'VE NEVER BEEN A fan of Saint Petersburg, a homogeneous city, petrified in time, and lacking the vital energy and constantly surprising forms that make Moscow so exciting and indecipherable. Every time I go, I have the impression of wandering through a stage set abandoned by its characters, the relic of a naive and grotesque wager that went wrong, a place quite justly relegated to the fringes of history. The tsar, on the other hand, feels completely at ease only when he's there. The moment he arrives in *Piter*, the cloak of maniacal self-control that envelops him in Moscow seems to slip to his feet, and a more affable character appears. That isn't to say he's suddenly all laughter and bonhomie, but in his hometown Putin relaxes and sometimes even has a beer or a glass of wine. Above all, Saint Petersburg is where his close friends and family are.

When I worked for the tsar, I sometimes traveled there to see him. I've never belonged to his intimate circle of friends. Our relationship, even in its most intense phases, has always been centered on work. There was something deeply anchored in our respective characters—and maybe also in our respective origins—that kept us from crossing over the threshold that normally leads to the dimension of friendship. And neither of us wanted to. Putin had his own crowd—his friends, the colorful and varied band of his fellow judo practitioners, the spies and wheeler-dealers with whom he had shared certain dark portions of his life before he came to the bright lights of the Kremlin. I had my books and I also now had Ksenia back, which was more than enough to satisfy my emotional needs. That said, he and I developed a true complicity over the years, and I don't think I'm wrong in saying that the tsar enjoyed my company. He liked to involve me in all sorts of different situations so as to hear my point of view. He knew that my response would be different from other people's and generally more direct. I think he saw me as someone with a certain inner freedom, and though it kept him from trusting me entirely, it also led him to seek my counsel. To be at his side was a great privilege for me. Not for the advantages it gave—the colored mirrors that attract the big predators and little carrion birds of politics—but for the unequaled experience of being able to follow him day after day, an Elizabethan drama playing itself out on the world's stage.

Putin was undeniably the main protagonist of that production, but the secondary roles constituted a dramatis personae worthy of *Richard III.* These were people who had gone from being provincial operators, bouncing checks and avoiding telephone calls from bank managers, to being within a few years the nobility of the empire, accumulating wealth on a scale comparable only to an emir from the Gulf States. The transformation, which happened very rapidly, swept everything in its path. Nothing of their original feelings or inclinations survived the torrent of billions that rained down on the tsar's friends. Each had been transformed to the very core of his being. But the implicit pact with Putin was to pretend that nothing had happened, to behave the same old way as ever. After all, it was because of the past that the tsar had showered them with gold, not for any exceptional talents they might have—and none of them did. While Putin did possess uncommon traits that justified his rise, their only merit consisted in having crossed his path at a particular moment and won his sympathy and, more importantly, his confidence. Managing to stay in the tsar's good graces was the one condition for keeping the manna falling abundantly from the sky. To do it, though, required more than a courtier's flattery. They were his friends from before, and Putin expected, or seemed to expect, a certain level of sincerity, though each of them also knew that that sincerity had its limits, imposed by the tsar's increasingly inflated opinion of himself. In practice, this meant offering the same praise as everyone else, but couched in the coarse banter of an old friend. This high-wire act led to some grotesque scenes, which I would sometimes witness in Petersburg. The old friends would trade jokes and proffer mild impertinences without ever crossing the tsar on any fundamental point, all vying to be the first to support his every idea.

It was on one of these occasions that I met Yevgeny Prigozhin. There were four or five of us in the private dining room of a restaurant amply supplied with mirrors and chandeliers. Putin introduced me to the owner, a bald, ordinary-looking man. He smiled modestly and kept up his role all through the meal, describing the different dishes, pouring the French *grand cru* wines, and generally making himself available to the tsar, attending to his gastronomic needs with dispatch. Wearing a silvery tie as though at a wedding, he spoke to us courteously, then, more sharply, to the waitstaff. Only at the end of the meal did Putin invite him to sit with us. The discussion at the table had shifted, as alcohol levels rose, to the relative merits of several European escort agencies. The tsar, who did not avail himself of their services, took no part in the discussion, but followed it with an amused expression—carefully monitored by all present, who were ready to discard the subject instantly should it change. Prigozhin joined in easily, his maître d's manner giving way to the jovial skepticism appropriate to members of the magic circle of Putin's longtime friends. He began with several racy stories about his nocturnal adventures in the Balearic Islands, which were much appreciated, then turned the discussion to his latest entrepreneurial venture, an enormous farming operation he had just bought on the shores of the Black Sea and intended to convert into an arugula farm. "You have no idea how hard it is to find decent arugula in Russia," he said, half-serious and half-jesting, as his tablemates teased him. But at a certain point, the tsar interrupted, turning to me.

"As you can tell, Yevgeny has quite a bit of initiative. He's also very interested in international affairs, and I think he could give us a hand with some issues we've been considering recently, isn't that so, Genia?"

At this, the restaurateur's eyes lit up. Putin continued: "It would be a good thing for the two of you to talk, Vadya."

You have to understand: the tsar never says anything specific, but he also never says anything at random. If he takes the trouble to make a suggestion, for instance, that his political advisor should meet with a Saint Petersburg restaurateur to discuss Russian foreign policy, then, crazy as it sounds, the idea has to be taken seriously and put into effect.

That night, Prigozhin invited me for the next day, never overstepping the role of gangster–cum–maître d' that he had been playing all night. But the next morning, when he came by the hotel to pick me up, I immediately realized he was more than a simple restaurateur. A brief car ride brought us to the port, where for an awful moment I thought he planned to take me on one of those sightseeing boats that try so hard to emulate the *bateaux-mouches* in Paris. Someone had told me that Prigozhin had business interests in this area too. Fortunately, however, we boarded a helicopter. "My house is not far, but I know you don't have much time to waste, Vadim Alexeievich. This way, it'll go faster."

At that hour, from above, with the fairy-tale facades of the palaces fronting on the canals, the reflections of the cupolas, and all the islands scattered across the Neva, the old capital shone like a death mask of marble and diamonds left to rot in the sun. To accompany the view, Prigozhin started telling me the epic tale of his relations with the tsar. It had been Putin, when he was deputy mayor of Saint Petersburg in the early 1990s, who had granted Prigozhin and a group of his partners the license to operate the first casino in the city. It must not have been an easy thing to pull off, given the times and the type of activity, but everything suggested that Prigozhin emerged from the venture to the good. From there began his ascension, which the tsar had watched over with unfailing goodwill.

The flight was brief and gave me no time to delve any deeper. After barely five minutes, we started our descent onto Kamenny Ostrov. I'd heard of the place, but I thought it was an exaggeration. People said that a group of the tsar's friends had bought themselves an island in Saint Petersburg where they lived like aristocrats from the imperial epoch in palaces covered in stucco and gold, and that they held fancy-dress balls that they attended dressed as courtiers of Alexander III. One of them apparently had even had his own coat of arms designed, with a profusion of lilies and rampant lions. As I looked down now at the meticulously restored villas of the former officials of the Russian Empire—the pools, sports houses, and gigantic garages, the moat that surrounded the island and the sentry boxes, the SUVs and the helicopters—I understood that, as is often the case in Russia, reality had once again surpassed all fiction.

"You know, I'm not an intellectual like you, Vadim Alexeievich. But I've learned a thing or two in my life."

Prigozhin was comfortably seated in a soi-disant Louis XVI chair with gold armrests. The Scandinavian furniture around him, the rearing lions, and the Murano candelabras were reflected in the white marble and enormous picture windows that looked out onto the Neva. The Uzbek decorator had done well.

"Do you know what a casino is, really? A monument to man's irrationality. If men were rational creatures, casinos wouldn't exist. Why in God's name would anyone agree to throw his money away in a place where all the odds are against him? But thank God men are not rational creatures, otherwise I'd never have come into any of this."

Prigozhin waved vaguely toward some paintings in the style of Basquiat and a white Steinway grand.

"There is no wiser course than to bet on man's folly."

—That's exactly right, Vadim Alexeievich. Do you know why some people lose their fortunes at the casino? Why they go headlong into a spiral they're unable to pull out of? Character has a role to play, of course, it doesn't happen to everyone. But these people aren't monsters. They may not be able to control themselves, but it's owing to a flaw in our brains, one that we all share.

Prigozhin stopped and fished a wallet out of the breast pocket of his jacket, from which he removed a five-thousand-ruble bill.

"Look at this. And try the experiment sometime with a random man on the street. Offer him a choice between this bill and a fifty percent chance of getting two bills like it. What's he going to do? I'll tell you: he'll take the bill. Now try the opposite. Ask a passerby either to *give* you five thousand rubles or else decide on a coin toss whether to give you two five-thousand-ruble bills or none at all. Do you know what he'll do this time? Rather than pay out five thousand rubles right away, he'll take the risk of having to pay you double. It's crazy, right? In theory, the person who stands to win could afford to take a risk, as opposed to the person who will be losing money. But people do the exact opposite instead. The ones who gain are more cautious in their choice, while the ones who lose bet the whole bankroll."

I looked at Prigozhin, who was beaming. I was starting to get a sense of where this was headed.

"The human brain is full of little quirks like that. Knowing them and figuring out how to profit from them is the business of the casino owner. But that's how politics works too, no? As long as you're secure and have a steady job, a family, a house in the country, vacations by the sea, retirement prospects, all of that, your mind is at rest. You make sensible choices, you don't want to run any risks. You choose what you already know. But let's say things start to deteriorate. The situation changes, the guy loses his job, loses his house, he can't look ahead into the future anymore. What does he do? Does he remain cautious? No, he starts to make crazy bets! He prefers an unknown risk to keeping things as they are. That's when you reach a tipping point: chaos becomes more attractive than order. Because at least it offers the chance of something new, right? In the theater, this would be called a dramatic turn of events. And that's when things start to get interesting. The Russian Revolution in 1917, Nazism—they grew out of just this kind of situation, am I right? Because a majority of people preferred to rush toward the unknown rather than go on living as before."

The Petersburg cook was flying a little high, but his proposals were far from uninteresting.

"Now, as I was telling you," he continued, "I'm not an intellectual or an expert in foreign relations, but I have the feeling that we've reached that point once more. In the West, people believe that their children will have a lower standard of living than they themselves had. They see giant progress in China, India, and, thank God, Russia, while they make none at all. With every passing day, their power diminishes, the situation slips further out of their control, the future is no longer theirs."

—They're ready to make crazy choices. We just have to help them do that.

—Precisely, Vadim Alexeievich. We don't need to convince them or force them in any way, just assist a movement that's already in progress. That's something the tsar understands very well. Like me, he loves judo, and he knows that its basic principle is to use your adversary's force against him.

Prigozhin's reasoning stopped there. To bear fruit, all it needed was a practical application. And I had an idea or two about that already up my sleeve.

We met again several weeks later, outside an ordinary-looking building on the outskirts of Petersburg. A suburban drizzle accentuated the sordidness of the area, but Prigozhin seemed in excellent humor.

"This is the place I was telling you about, Vadim Alexeievich, you'll see..."

We rode up in an elevator and emerged into a large, computer-filled space, part newsroom of a daily paper, part trading room of a second-tier investment bank. Except that along one wall Prigozhin had installed two slot machines—in tribute to the spirit of the place, as he confided. And why not? After all, there are Ping-Pong tables at Google's offices, or so I've heard.

An athletic young man greeted us with a smile. He was wearing a collared shirt and corduroy jacket, as though about to lead a graduate seminar at Georgetown University.

"I'd like you to meet Anton," said Prigozhin, clearly proud of his discovery. "I chose him to lead the editorial department. He has a doctorate in international relations from Moscow University and speaks English, French, and German. He knows more about European politics than most of our government representatives."

Anton listened quietly. His expression betrayed neither pride nor false modesty. We started by talking about everything and nothing. I then decided to test him on the domestic situation in some of our neighboring European countries. Not only was Anton brilliant, but I found him very appealing. He had none of the arrogance that afflicts so many of his overprotected generation. In fact, there was a directness about him that is always the sign of a truly superior intelligence. His understanding of the international situation was as sharp as a hunting knife. He could enter into the details without ever losing sight of the general picture.

Prigozhin watched him, smiling happily. His protégé was making him proud. After a minute or two, I'd had enough. I took leave of Anton, shaking his hand, and led Prigozhin aside. I was bowled over by his stupidity.

"What is going through your mind, Yevgeny?"

The cook's face darkened.

"Is there something wrong, Vadim Alexeievich?"

—What could you have possibly been thinking? I thought I'd made it clear: we want to affect politics in Europe and the United States. Take part in the debate, make our contribution to it. And you bring me this kid?

He gestured toward Anton: "But he's very good. He knows everything."

—Exactly, Yevgeny, that's the whole problem.

Prigozhin raised his eyebrows in such an exaggerated expression of perplexity that I burst out laughing.

"Think, Yevgeny. Westerners have no interest in politics. If we want to draw their attention, we have to talk about anything but politics. We don't need Anton here! What we need is young women giving beauty tips, video game nerds, astrologers, people like that, get it?"

—But at a certain point, we'll need to convey your message, no? You'll issue directives...

—Who do you take us for, the Comintern? I'm sorry to have to tell you, but the Soviet Union is over and done with, there is no working-class paradise on the horizon. Those times are gone forever. There's no line, Yevgeny, only steel wire.

His look of confusion prompted me to continue.

"When you want to break a piece of steel wire, what do you do? You twist it first in one direction, then in the other. That's what we'll do, Yevgeny. As you build up your networks, you'll find issues that people really care about. I don't know what they are, but the clicks will tell you. Maybe there's somebody who's against vaccines, somebody else who's against hunters, or environmentalists, or Blacks, or whites. It doesn't matter. What's important is that there's something every person feels strongly about, and someone who really makes them angry.

"We don't need to convert anyone, Yevgeny. We just need to find out what they believe and convince them of it even more, is that starting to make sense? Pumping out the news, broadcasting true arguments or false, none of that has any importance. But making them mad, all of them. Madder and madder. The animal rights people on one side and the hunters on the other. The Black Power people, and the white supremacists. The LGBTQ activists and the neo-Nazis. We have no preferences, Yevgeny. The only line we follow is the line of steel wire. We bend it to one side and we bend it to the other. Until it breaks."

Prigozhin looked at me for a long moment in silence. He was thinking.

"OK, Vadya, I've got it. The line of steel wire. But what's going to happen when they catch on to us? Because you know that's going to happen, right? Everything on the internet can be traced. And we're playing on their home field. They'll realize it sooner or later. They're going to drag us through the mud and worse."

—Just the opposite, Yevgeny. That will be our moment of victory.

Silence.

"You don't see it? The ultimate gesture that a great artist makes is to reveal contradiction! They expect us to support pro-Russian sympathizers and anti-American groups, right? But what will they do when they realize that we're also supporting their political opponents? The patriotic Second Amendment guys who want to take their semiautomatic pistols with them, even into the bathroom. The vegans who'd sooner drink hemlock than a glass of milk. The young people who want to save the world from environmental disaster. I'll tell you. They'll go crazy, they won't know what's going on. They won't know who to believe or what to believe anymore! The only thing they'll understand is that we've gotten inside their heads and are playing with their neural networks as if they were slot machines!"

A smile finally appeared on Prigozhin's face. He was starting to understand.

"That's why the main point of this place is to be discovered, Yevgeny. To get caught. Do you really think that a hundred kids in a place like this can change history? Of course not. No matter how good they are, it's not going to happen. They'll just ride the chaos, maybe succeed in increasing it a bit, but the anger that they'll harness already exists, and the algorithm that controls it was invented by the Americans, not the Russians. We'll just prick them with our spurs, that's all. But we'll allow ourselves to be caught red-handed! And that will be the decisive moment. Our accusers will be the ones to say that we are plotting against democracy, in Europe and the United States. They will be the ones to build the myth of our power. All we have to do is to act suspiciously and come up with a few fairly implausible denials. That will be enough to confirm their worst nightmare: 'The Russians are the secret bosses of the new world order!' And this midnight fantasy will, in turn, increase the chaos. Our power will go from being a myth to a reality. That's what's nice about politics, Yevgeny: anything that makes people believe in power actually increases that power."

25

BEREZOVSKY LUMBERED LIKE A dinosaur through the phosphorescent lighting of Claridge's. A tipsy giraffe in a Celine pantsuit turned to follow him with her eyes. Even an American, there on a layover, seemed to notice the incongruity of this prehistoric presence among so much mahogany and sparkling crystal. Or else he recognized him. Boris had been involved in so many scandals and provocations that he'd started to become a recognizable face among the Georgian houses in Mayfair. We'd fallen into the habit of meeting whenever I happened to be traveling through London. I had long ago stopped having any more messages to deliver to him. And maybe because of that, the simple pleasure of spending a few hours together had become the sole reason for our get-togethers. On my part, anyway. As happens to intelligent people who fall from power, Berezovsky had become, if not wiser, at least more lucid. And on that night I remember that I complimented him on his impeccable British accent.

"What do you expect? Your ancestors spoke French and took refuge in Paris, whereas the modern-day Russian speaks English and finds comfort in London!"

He smiled a little sadly, then suddenly shook himself.

"Don't imagine that the English are always easy to deal with. Last week I was in the office of a banker to sign a contract with the brother of a sheikh from the Gulf. We started to produce our documents, when do you know what this bank employee did? He asked the sheikh for his ID card. The sheikh looked around, turned to his staff—he's not in the habit of carrying his wallet when he goes out. I tried to intercede, but the bank man was one of those rigid bastards you sometimes find around here.

"I was afraid the sheikh might suddenly get angry and drop the whole business. But do you know what he did? He had his assistant give him a banknote, which he held out to the banker. The man looks at him in disbelief: 'What on earth are you doing? Are you offering me a tip? That may be an acceptable custom in your country, but not in the City.' 'Look carefully,' says the sheikh. 'What's printed on this banknote is my face. I hope that's enough of a document for you.' Everyone burst out laughing, and in the end the bastard bank guy had to give in."

Fortunately, Boris's talent for entertaining the troops while at the same time singing his own praises had not diminished. Unfortunately, his obsessions hadn't changed either.

"How are things going with Putin's Games?"

—The preparations for the Winter Olympics are going quite well, thank you. The president was kind enough to put me in charge of the opening ceremony. There will be a major show before the athletic contests begin.

—Hmm, sounds good. I hope you've also organized a medal for the biggest ass-kisser. And a medal for killing, awarded to the best GRU assassin.

—I don't know, maybe, Boris. The important thing is for Russia to come out ahead of everyone else.

—That shouldn't be a problem, I'm sure you'll find a solution, as you usually do.

Berezovsky paused, then resumed. "He'll never stop, will he? People like him can't. It's the first rule. Keep going. Don't correct a thing if it's worked before, but especially never admit to any mistakes. At first I didn't understand, but I've now had the time to think about it. I've also read a ton of books about earlier dictators. So, for example, do you know what Mobutu did when he came into power in the Congo? He renamed the country Zaire because he thought it was a native term, a way of shaking off the colonial past. Then it came out that Zaire is a Portuguese word. So what does he do? Does he apologize and reverse course? Not on your life! He plasters "Zaire" on everything else too: on banknotes, cigarettes, gas pumps, even on condoms, for all I know... Your tsar is exactly the same: an autocrat, a tribal chief!"

—It could be, Boris, but it's not barbarism—that's how the game is played. The first rule of power is to forge ahead with your mistakes, never to show the slightest crack in the wall of authority. Mobutu knew it because he came from a place where in the old days the chieftain was killed if he even fell from his horse. And he'd be strangled to death if he became ill. The chieftain has to be strong if he's to protect his people. The moment he shows any weakness, he's killed and replaced by somebody else. It's the same everywhere. But depending on where you are, the deposed chieftain can be impaled on a stake or sent to the far end of the world to give speeches at a hundred thousand dollars a shot.

Berezovsky assumed a thoughtful expression, deepened by the bar's dark shadows and dim light.

"You're right, Vadya, but remember that there's no *happy ending* in politics. Even the Sun King, at the end of his life, had terrible crying spells."

—What can I say, Boris? Life is a fatal disease.

—Exactly, Vadya. And that's precisely why you have to recognize when the moment comes to cut the crap. I've always thought one of the things that politics has in common with the mob is that you don't retire from it. You can't pull out of politics and start doing something else. Then I came across Johnny Torrio. Do you know his story, Vadya, the story of Johnny Torrio?

I shook my head. I already had a foretaste of this umpteenth parable of Berezovsky's, even if, at the time, I didn't know it would be his last.

—He was the boss of the mob syndicate in Chicago just after World War I, a real leader, respected by all. But one of his subordinates was a man who wanted to take his place, a man called Al Capone. So in 1924, one afternoon in January, around five o'clock, Johnny Torrio, the president of the Chicago Mafia council, collapses across the street from his house with five bullet holes in his body. They take him to the hospital, he says to the police: "I know who did it, but I'm not a rat." Then, when he got better, he called on Al Capone, gave him the keys to his business, and told him he wanted to return to Italy. The upshot was that he lived another fifteen years and, by the grace of God, died peacefully in his Brooklyn home.

Boris was silent for a moment, then he pulled a letter from his pocket.

"This letter is for the tsar. I wrote it from the heart. You can read it if you like."

The paper was handmade and felt to the touch like a square of cotton fabric. It was an appeal to the tsar's Christian mercy. "I implore you in Christ's name to pardon me," Berezovsky had written. Then there were some tear-jerking allusions to his approaching death, to the sorrows of exile, to an old fool who, cognizant of his past errors, entreated his sovereign, whose magnanimity he trusted entirely, for permission to spend his remaining days in the arms of the motherland. It didn't rise to the tone of Zamyatin's letter. More of a supplication, in the pure style of a long secular tradition. Even if, in one passage, Boris had succumbed to the temptation of proposing himself as an advisor "on the basis of my accumulated experience, if you thought it might be useful, Vladimir Vladimirovich."

"Do you think it will work?"

The old ruffian queried me fervently, while trying for an ironic expression, but what I read in his eyes was a bottomless despair. I wanted to tell him: Yes, the tsar will be moved, we will soon be standing side by side in the president's box to review the opening parade of the Sochi Games. What flashed through my mind was that within days, Berezovsky would forget his earnest proposals and be champing at the bit once more, making suggestions and demanding to be given a role. I missed his energy. He was no saint, but in everything he undertook there was a kind of joy. Since his banishment, and the banishment of so many others of his kind, Moscow had been left with nothing but the glum determination of the *siloviki*. But I knew that the tsar didn't hanker for his return, far from it. Boris read the answer in my eyes, even if he wasn't ready to accept it.

"Well, take it with you anyway. I think it might work."

We parted that night with a Russian bear hug, prolonged to the point that it started to disturb the refined ambience of Claridge's. I went up to my room weighed down by a strange sense of defeat. In the final analysis, the old lion had agreed to pull the taxi driver's beret down over his eyes. It proved once again that the weakness you don't know but might suspect waits in the shadows like a reptile in a bush and can emerge at any point, right up to the end, even when you might be thinking that you've led your life without ever having to bend your neck.

Two days after our meeting, Berezovsky was found dead in the bathroom of his Ascot home, hanged with his favorite cashmere scarf.

26

"THE PROBLEM IS NOT that man is mortal, but that he's unexpectedly mortal."

At any other time, I'd have been thrilled that the tsar had gone to the trouble of exhuming Bulgakov for me. But that day I was not inclined to appreciate literary quotations. Naturally, Putin realized this.

"You really think we did it?"

The tsar's face was a sheet of granite. I cast a glance around me. I hated the officialness and desolation of Novo-Ogaryovo, its mix of false intimacy and authentic bad taste, as though the job of decorating the president's residence on the outskirts of Moscow had been given at some point to the Kremlin's chief of security. Which may in fact have happened. Even under normal circumstances the bronze standing lamps and damask-covered walls saddened me. I felt it all the more this morning, when the newspapers were brimming with the news of Boris's death and his vain entreaty was burning the breast pocket of my jacket like a bullet in a wound.

"I don't think anything, Mister President."

—And you'd be entirely right, Vadya.

The tsar allowed a few moments to pass for the deeper meaning of his warning to penetrate beyond my cortex into the central regions of my brain. Then he resumed, in a more worldly tone: "In any case, the truth is that Berezovsky was very useful for us. Every time he opened his mouth to say that he'd be back once I was no longer in power, it worked to our advantage. People remembered the 1990s, all that suffering, that chaos. You only had to look at him for what he was."

When I maintained my stubborn silence, Putin continued. "Of course, it's true he was helping Russia's enemies all over the place. In Ukraine, in Latvia, in Georgia. Who knows what really happened? You see, Vadya, conspiracy theorists think they're incredibly clever, but really they're big dolts. They'd like everything to have a hidden meaning, and they systematically underestimate the power of stupidity, of carelessness, of chance. That said, more power to them: it's not what they want, but conspiracy theorists benefit us. If instead of seeing power as it really is, with all its human weakness, you give it an aura of omniscience, an ability to hatch plots of every kind, then you're doing it the biggest favor possible, no? You're making people think it's greater than it is."

—"As these mysteries are beyond us," I quoted in the original French, "let us pretend to have originated them."

The tsar hated it when I spouted literary quotations, and he didn't speak French, but I was in no mood to humor him that morning. He looked at me for a moment in silence, then decided to move on.

"It was the same with those other cases: the colonel, the lawyer, the famous lady journalist. You know it perfectly well, Vadya, it wasn't us. We never do anything. We just create the conditions that allow for various possibilities."

It could well have been true. For a long time, the tsar hadn't given direct orders, or only rarely. He'd go as far as to set the boundaries, what was allowable and what was not. The game then followed its own logic, right up to the most extreme consequences, which also constituted its deepest truth. This was exactly what Berezovsky and I had talked about a few days earlier— a coincidence whose irony in no way made me want to smile. It would more likely have made me cry, if I'd been able to. The idea that in the end the old bandit only wanted to finish out his life like Johnny Torrio touched me much more than I'd have thought. Poor Borya, he'd certainly have deserved to.

Across from me, the tsar was reading Berezovsky's letter. He set it down, imperturbable, as if he were a stone on a riverbed. I realized then that Boris had been right on this point too, that Putin wasn't a great actor, as I'd thought, only a great spy. The calling is a schizophrenic one, and it undoubtedly requires a certain talent as an actor. But a true actor is extroverted, he takes real pleasure in communicating. A spy, on the other hand, has to know how to block his emotions, if he has any in the first place. In practice, both talents serve the spy. He must simulate the actor's empathy while having the icy detachment of a surgeon in the operating room. But if Putin was not a great actor, I was not a great director either. An accomplice, at best.

That day, rather than linger over Boris's fate, the tsar turned the conversation to the preparations for the Olympic Games in Sochi. It was his obsession at the time. In order to convince the Olympic Committee to hold the Winter Games in a subtropical town without any infrastructure or transportation facilities, Putin had mobilized all the might of contemporary Russia and some of the manipulative fantasy-building of his earlier life. At a certain point, a group of Olympic inspectors came to visit, and as Sochi had no airport, one was counterfeited. Students dressed as tourists stared at signboards that posted the departure and arrival times of nonexistent flights. Potemkin would have been proud of us.

The closer we came to the Games' opening day, the harder the tsar found it to talk about anything else. It was clear that he considered hosting the Games to be the high point of his reign. And I have to admit that I found it fascinating to take part in them as the person responsible for the opening ceremony. My career was, at this point, coming full circle. I'd started out in the theater and gone from there to directing reality. No one can say I didn't do a good job. Now I was being asked to project onto the stage the reality I'd helped create. Only this time it wasn't at a little avant-garde theater but in an enormous arena, for an audience spanning the entire planet.

This was the occasion I'd been waiting for. Impersonating a minor god, I'd gone down a dead-end road. What I wanted now was to turn around and come back, to reestablish a relationship with everything I'd found beautiful in the world. So I was being commissioned to put Russia on the stage, the tragic greatness of its history, the poignant beauty of its songs and writings? Very well, I'd make it a personal story, an opportunity to reknit the broken threads of my family, which were, in point of fact, the broken threads of every Russian family.

In my generation, we'd seen our fathers humiliated. They were serious, conscientious men who'd worked hard all their lives, and then, in their last few years, found themselves as bewildered as an Australian aborigine trying to cross the expressway. This applied to the children of the *nomenklatura* as much as to anyone else. We'd seen our parents, strong figures, our points of reference, wandering with staring eyes, shocked at the collapse of everything they'd believed in. We saw them mocked and vilified for having simply done their

duty. In truth, we were the ones who mocked and vilified them. We were all of us shaken to the core by this
spectacle. We'd brought it about, and we were shaken
by it. Afterwards, no one's conscience was clean. Now,
though, we wanted to do right by them. By them and
by their fathers, whom they, too, had humiliated, because Russia is condemned always to repeat itself.

Through the years, the tsar had patiently gathered
the threads of Russian history to give it a degree of
coherence. The Russia of Alexander Nevsky, the patri-
archs' Third Rome, the Russia of Peter the Great, the
Russia of Stalin, and the Russia of today. Putin's own
greatness showed in this, but he'd afterwards given in
to the temptation of finding in brute force the through
line he was seeking—a dark progression, if not without
greatness, from the *oprichniki* of Ivan the Terrible, by
way of the tsar's secret police and Stalin's cheka, to the
Sechins and Prigozhins of today.

Given his origins, it may not have been possible for
the tsar to do otherwise. But the *siloviki* had contributed nothing to the beauty of the world, their stories
were not meant to be told but rather to be hushed up.
In their hands, whatever was marvelous or tragic in
Russian history would appear in a harsh light, as an
uninterrupted succession of abuse and sacrifice. What
was being asked of us now was to relate what our
Russian history had contributed to the world's store of
beauty. Something the Sechins and Prigozhins knew

nothing about. And Putin himself, I think, would not have known where to start.

I, on the other hand, thought I did know. More particularly, I knew where to look: in the bookcases of my grandfather's library, in his hunting stories, in the novels my father had reread in the months before his death, and in the complex genealogy of madmen and artists Ksenia and I had absorbed in our youth, back when Moscow had been a multicolored mirage.

I decided to call on my friends from those days. Many were unwilling to sign on; some bridled at being co-opted by the system, while others, though willing enough to be co-opted, refused to contribute to a mega-production that, as they said, had every chance of being in horribly bad taste. They were right, in a way. The scale of the production dictated the mode of expression: it would have to be kitsch, which is the only language that can reliably communicate with the masses, because it simplifies everything and avoids nuance. But nowhere was it written that kitsch couldn't itself be subverted and turned to my own ends.

We set to work. Funds were unlimited. The tsar was not going to hold back when it came to projecting his greatness across the surface of the globe. We picked the best in every category and had fun putting it all together. The costume designers drew on tradition for our characters' clothes, but also on the sketches of a Japanese fashion designer. The choreographers staged

the Stalinist era in a grandiose style by drawing on the
constructivists, whom the Little Father abhorred. The
vast open-space studio that I'd had outfitted for our
creative team—just outside the walls of the Kremlin, so
that I could go there as often as possible—reminded me
a little of my time as a television producer. Some of the
faces that turned up there were the same, but fifteen
years older. And even the others, the younger set that
joined us, all had a family look. From long experience
I'd grown adept at sifting through the faces of people
with thick-framed glasses, faded T-shirts, and 1970s
quartz watches, looking for the tiniest glint of true
gold. Our young collaborators all had the spark that
distinguishes real talent from the abject mass of cocktail creatives, though it could be hard from the outside
to tell them apart from the spoiled youngsters who
gathered in the bistros of central Moscow to plan flash
mobs in support of the tsar's opponents. Their dishev-
eled hair and purple corduroy jackets clashed with the
usual denizens of the Kremlin's halls. I could understand why the minister of culture, a standard-bearer for
traditional values who'd been assigned to oversee the
preparations, had started to show signs of nervousness.
Like most other members of Putin's court, he'd always
disapproved of my activities, which sometimes inter-
sected with his, almost always to countervail them. So
many subversives of all different stripes, he thought,
couldn't possibly lead to anything good. And this guy

Baranov, he mused, is he really manipulating them or is he fundamentally one of theirs?

As long as my relationship with the tsar was unassailable, there wasn't much he could do, but now that it was starting to show cracks—nothing escaped the hypersensitive antennae of the courtiers—it might be the moment to step in. When he learned that some of us were floating the idea of having the Red Army Choir perform a song by Daft Punk, the minister decided to appeal to Sechin. And that's why I found myself once again in the tsar's office.

Sechin, standing at his usual post behind the tsar, who was seated at his desk, lost no time in getting to the point.

"Vadya is turning the ceremony into a farce. He's brought together all his Moscow cronies, and they're planning to make fools of us."

From the start, Igor had always worn his total lack of humor as a badge of trustworthiness. The tsar answered him distractedly.

"And what can we do about it, Igor? Our friend Vadya is an acrobat. Among bankers, he's an artist; among artists, a banker. You can never catch up with him because he's always somewhere else."

Sechin looked at me with the expression of a dentist about to inflict pain. "Watch out, Vadya, because sooner or later you're going to miss your trapeze and come crashing to the ground."

In a way, he was right, but I wasn't ready to concede, not yet.

"Sorry, Igor, but don't you have any traitors to the fatherland to impale? Because we're trying to work on a show here, OK? The greatest show ever produced."

Sechin looked at me for a moment in astonishment. It had been years since anyone had dared speak to him that way, aside from the tsar. He was so surprised he didn't even manage to get angry.

The tsar seemed amused. He always liked it when his subordinates squabbled. I turned to him once more.

"Mister President, three billion people will be watching this performance. Most of them don't know anything about our country. All they know is that at one point there were Reds, but now there aren't. That's the sum total, let's not kid ourselves. We have two hours to introduce them to our Russia. The Russia that we've built, and the Russia we're striving for. We can show them an advanced country, one that doesn't have any complexes, that assimilates the outside world and reflects it, that influences the world and is influenced by it. A Russia that is open, sure of itself, and that inspires awe because of its great destiny but that can also make you smile, because you need a certain amount of humor to deal with today's world. Or, of course, we could spend two hours entertaining them with babushkas in traditional costume and Igor's military choirs."

Putin has his faults, but he's certainly capable of evaluating people for what they are and, more particularly, for how they can be useful to him in achieving his ends. On any other project, he'd have sided with Sechin, who was more trustworthy, more obedient, and more efficient. But for mounting a show that the whole world would see, he had the good sense to choose me. Doubtless it would be for the last time, Sechin would see to that. But what mattered for the moment was to be able to finish the work.

During this period, I took advantage of being in the tsar's favor to ask if he might grant me something close to my heart: Mikhail's freedom. The idea that Ksenia had returned to me because Mikhail was out of the running tormented me. I needed to go up against him on an equal footing. I knew now that I could do it. I was no longer the perpetual student who hid behind a barricade of books to avoid dealing with life: I'd stopped lying to myself, gone out into the world, killed my first goose and many more; I was at the top of my game. Ksenia had sensed it. That's why she'd come back to me. And that's why she'd stay. Mikhail's release from prison was the one thing that was needed to ensure this.

There were numerous arguments in favor of releasing him. After the first trial, he'd served his time at the Krasnokamensk camp in the middle of a Martian landscape of red, powdery hills on the far boundary between Siberia and China. There he'd given proof of courage and dignity. He may simply have been too presumptuous not to be extremely brave as well. One time, he'd gone on a hunger strike to get medical care for an ex-employee of his company who was imprisoned with him and was HIV positive. After ten days, the prosecutor had had to give in. Another time, he'd managed to get better working conditions for his cellmates, who spent their days in the camp's sewing workshop.

Now, his mother was ill—the doctors gave her at most a year to live. Releasing him would be an act of compassion. The tsar knew this. Russians like their leaders to be implacable, but they also approve of an occasional act of clemency. Then, too, it was a question of self-assurance for the tsar. Having spent years consolidating his unlimited power, did he not feel strong enough to show magnanimity toward an adversary who had, in fact, shown himself worthy of respect?

I obviously couldn't formulate the question in exactly these terms, but I managed things so that Putin saw the question more or less this way. I did, after working with him for years, have a vague idea of how to influence his thought processes. I wasn't always successful. But this time I was. And so, a few days before the start of the Olympic Games, the tsar announced the release of Khodorkovsky, just as Caesar had once pardoned Claudius Marcellus.

Ksenia rushed to the prison gates to be on hand when Mikhail emerged. She put him on his plane, accompanied him to Berlin, where his parents lived, and stayed with him for several days to make sure he was fit to resume normal life. Then she announced that she was filing for divorce.

It may have been the first time since I'd known her that Ksenia had behaved exactly as I'd expected. This was a woman who would burn down a whole city to spare herself a moment of tedium. Yet I found in her nearness a kind of peace that I'd never have found in the company of more tranquil natures. Before she'd chosen me, Ksenia had betrayed and wounded me, as she'd betrayed and wounded any number of other men. If she'd decided to lay down her weapons, it wasn't from lassitude or cowardice. On the contrary, it was because she'd fought and won too many battles.

It's not enough in life for two people to recognize each other, it has to happen at the right moment, when they are both ready to celebrate the silent communion that will unite them. We were happy together and happy also at the prospect of the unknown future before us. For now, all we needed to do was to enjoy the opening ceremony. The show promised to be spectacular.

27

THE MASKED MEN MADE their entrance suddenly, goose-stepping to the powerful rhythm of drums that echoed in the darkness. Holding flashlights, they quickly formed into a swastika in the middle of the stadium. Then they started throwing rocks and Molotov cocktails at the policemen. The police defended themselves as best they could, but were clearly getting the worst of it, and when the armored Ukrainian vehicles arrived, with their flags clearly visible, the policemen were eliminated, down to the last man. A familiar voice came blasting from the loudspeakers: "Eternal lackeys of Europe! Spiritual slaves of America! You have perverted the history of your fathers and sold the graves of your ancestors! You have burned and bloodied Ukraine to carry out Adolf Hitler's plan!"

Meanwhile, two gigantic mechanical hands, painted in the colors of the American flag, lifted a model of

Ukraine in flames into the air. "You value a foreign country more highly than your homeland, and for that reason you are fated to recognize no voice but your master's and to prostrate yourselves before him forevermore! But you forgot to take Russia into account!"

At this point, a phalanx of Russian patriots burst into the arena and started battling the Nazis and the Ukrainian soldiers. Flashes of light, explosions, bodies falling to the ground. In the smoke and darkness, the outcome of the battle wasn't clear. Until the Night Wolves roared into the arena astride their motorcycles, brandishing the Russian flag, while the national anthem blared. When the fog lifted, the Nazis were lying on the ground in a lake of blood, and the loudspeakers played the tsar's recorded voice: "The nationalists, neo-Nazis, Russia haters, and anti-Semites stopped at nothing in their effort to seize power. They resorted to terror, assassination, and riots. But how could they think we'd ignore Ukraine's citizens when they implored us for help? We couldn't, it would have been a betrayal! Because Russia and Ukraine are not just neighbors, as we've often said, they are one people! Kiev is the mother of the Russian nation. We both descend from ancient Rus, and we cannot live without one another. We have done much together, but much remains to be done, new challenges remain to be addressed. I'm certain that we'll overcome all obstacles, we will succeed because we are united! Long live Russia! Long live the Russian people!"

The show ended with an orgy of flamethrowers and industrial exhalations, with lasers piercing the shadows and the deafening sound of industrial fans overlaying the heavy metal from the gigantic speakers around the edges of the stadium. The wind off the Eastern mountains shook the flags of the separatists and an enormous banner: "Where you find the Night Wolves, there you find Russia." In a transport of enthusiasm, a member of the audience fired his Kalashnikov into the sky, while most of the spectators watched dumbfounded, with the confused look of people who have temporarily lost their sense of hearing.

I have to admit that I, too, was a little stunned. A few months earlier, the opening ceremony of the Olympic Winter Games had been a triumph. The set pieces had summoned up the major eras in Russia's history, the onion domes of St. Basil's Cathedral had risen into view, to the spectators' delight. Natasha and Prince Andrei had danced at the imperial court, and a blond child, suspended in space on a blue globe, had finally released the red balloon of Communism. The strains of Stravinsky's *Firebird* accompanied the passing of the Olympic torch, and the Red Army Choir had sung "Get Lucky." I returned to the hotel that night feeling that I'd finally found my way into the clear after a long journey. For a few hours at least, I'd created a world of enchantment.

The show that I was presently watching was somewhat different. It looked like the set for an apocalyptic movie. The flickering gas jets illuminated a moonscape strewn with the hulks of cars, among which metallic centaurs moved, slowly ebbing from the stadium. The headquarters of the Luhansk Night Wolves appeared in the background, its walls topped with barbed wire.

"So, Vadya, how about it, did you like the show?"

The thunderous voice that had highlighted key moments of the spectacle only moments before was now addressing me. Zaldostanov had moved to the Donbas some time earlier, to be in the front lines of the patriotic war for Eastern Ukraine. The tsar obviously couldn't send regular troops to invade a sovereign country. We'd therefore assembled a strange army of mercenaries and soldiers in civilian clothing. Officially, these good people were all volunteers, veterans of Afghanistan and Chechnya, who had decided to spend their vacation defending Russian-speaking Ukrainians from the Nazis of Maidan Square. Although they lacked the beaver-fur berets and cinch-waisted black tunics of the nineteenth-century Cossacks, they were otherwise indistinguishable from them.

Alexander had assumed their command in the role of charismatic leader. Tanned and newly trim, he struck me as being in his element. It didn't surprise me. At moments of turbulence, Russia has always produced men of this type—adventurers, leaders of small bands, characters who rise out of nowhere to spearhead history's upheavals. Alexander was of their kind. The world he loved was a world without rules, a place where things happened, and that was that. His followers worshipped him as if the god of war had materialized in front of their eyes. They all shared a sense of euphoria at being able to grab a weapon and obtain all the things they were forbidden in times of peace. Sunglasses were their style, as were all-terrain vehicles without license plates, beards, tattoos, pounding music, and semiautomatic weapons.

Zaldostanov, who had mounted the show to celebrate Russia's imminent victory in Eastern Ukraine, joined me in the wings. I complimented him on his interpretation of the god Thor. Alexander thanked me modestly. He moved with precision: a nod from him caused a bottle of vodka to appear, in a plastic ice bucket, alongside a plate of smoked herring and several thick slices of black bread.

"Alexander, dear friend, you know I've always imagined great things for you, ever since we met up again. But to find you like this, a Roman proconsul..."

—You know what they say, Vadya: "Those fated to hang don't die by drowning."

The biker knocked back a glass of vodka. Then he went on: "But what about you, my friend, they tell me you've reproduced. About time!"

—Not quite yet. In a few weeks, if all goes well. A girl, God willing.

Clearly, Zaldostanov had well-informed contacts in Moscow. Then again, Russians are extraordinarily resourceful when it comes to finding pretexts for a toast.

"Did you notice the flags? We don't use the Russian Federation flag anymore: we're thinking of replacing it."

During the performance I had in fact noticed that the bikers were waving ancient imperial banners with the two-headed eagle, one of Zaldostanov's obsessions.

"We're no longer a republic, Vadya, we've become an empire again. We're conquering new lands, and we already have a tsar to lead us: His Imperial Majesty Vladimir Putin!"

We downed another toast. Zaldostanov went on, "I want to thank you for visiting, Vadya. I really wanted to talk to you: I think the time has come to plot out the next stages."

I repressed a smile. Zaldostanov wanted to plot out the next stages: the two-headed eagle must have pecked holes in his brain.

"At this point, I think we have two options. The first and best would be to do what we did in Crimea. We organize a referendum, and then, in a wave of public fervor, the Donbas becomes part of Mother Russia again. The tsar notches up another conquest to go with the rest, and we're one step closer to rebuilding the Russian Empire..."

—And the other?

—The second option is not as good. But if it can't be done any other way, then we announce the independence of the Republic of Donbas. You guys in Moscow recognize the new state, as do a few others, maybe Belarus and Turkmenistan. We create a government, a parliament, we put our men in there, and then we coordinate on the steps to take after that.

—Hmm, I think we're going to have to opt for a third possibility, Alexander.

Zaldostanov looked at me, puzzled.

"Sorry," I went on, "but you seem to have gotten ahead of yourself."

—What are you talking about? I'm right here on the ground, and I'm only telling you what we need to do in order to consolidate our victory.

—That's just it, Alexander. Our victory. I'm afraid there's been a misunderstanding on this point.

Zaldostanov looked at me with vague hostility.

"The leaders of the local militia don't understand," I continued. "They pursue naive objectives, like victory. But you're not that stupid, are you, Alexander? You understand that war is a process, and that its goals extend far beyond military success. The fact is that it's important for us never to succeed completely, never to let our conquest become definitive. What would Russia do with two new regions? We took back Crimea because it was ours, but our motivation here is different. What we're aiming for is not conquest but chaos. The world has to see that the Orange Revolution plunged Ukraine into anarchy. If you make the mistake of trusting the West, that's how it always ends. The West drops you at the first bump in the road, and you're left all on your own to deal with a demolished country."

And a country overrun with barbarian hordes, I might have added. But I was still trying to tread softly around my host's sensitivities.

"This war is not being fought in the real world, Alexander, it's being fought in people's heads. The importance of your actions on the battlefield isn't measured by the number of towns you've taken, but by the number of brains you've conquered. Not here, but in Moscow, in Kiev, in Berlin. Think of all our compatriots in Russia who, thanks to you, have recovered a heroic sense of life, a belief in the struggle between good and evil. Think how much they admire the tsar, who is defending our values against Ukraine's Nazis and the West's decadence. Russian youths never experienced the chaos of the 1990s, and someone has to remind them that Putin is the embodiment of stability and the greatness of the motherland. Think also of the Ukrainians who, thanks to you, understand what a mistake they made: they were hoping that the Orange Revolution would be their ticket into Europe, when it's actually brought them back to the Middle Ages, to anarchy and perpetual violence. And think of the Westerners who, thanks to you, have learned to respect and fear Russia again. They thought that history had ended, and now they can see how badly they were mistaken. We haven't forgotten what it means to be men, to fight, to be ready to die. We aren't afraid to get our hands dirty. There's a big difference between living and trying not to die. They've forgotten that, but we haven't. We're here to remind them, Alexander.

"And all this is thanks to you. To you personally and to all the heroes who are waging war in the Donbas. But you need to understand that you're actors in a drama that's bigger than what happens here and extends far beyond the battlefield."

—For just how long?

Despite often using it to his advantage, or maybe because of it, Zaldostanov had always been impervious to the power of rhetoric.

"As long as it continues to be useful to us."

Zaldostanov was silent for a moment. "A drama, you call it? It looks more like a farce to me, Vadya. You think I don't know what's happening? People here have been talking about your little trips to Kiev. We know what you're trying to do. You're using us as a means to exert pressure. You want the Donbas region to stay a part of Ukraine, because you can use it to blackmail the government in Kiev."

I tried to maintain my composure, but the idea of this ape poking his nose into matters that were beyond his competence was starting to aggravate me.

"It won't work, Vadya, you're going to lose control. Our men here didn't take up arms to let you play your little political games in Kiev. They're fighting for their country, they want to see the birth of Novorussia. When they find out you're using them as bargaining chips to negotiate with the Nazis in Kiev..."

—Yes, what's going to happen, Alexander? Tell me, I'm curious to know.

I'd been unable to restrain myself. Zaldostanov kept quiet.

"I'll tell you: absolutely nothing. You seem to have fallen for the play you just staged. Might I ask you, Alexander, where you got the money for this farce, as we've agreed to call it?"

Zaldostanov scowled.

"From Moscow."

—And the weapons, where do they come from?

—From Moscow.

—And the hookers? Even the hookers are sent to you from Moscow, when we think you deserve them. So, one of two things will happen, Alexander. Either you're going to continue enjoying the position of good fortune you've parachuted into, thanks to me as it happens, or you're going to decide that no, it doesn't work for you anymore. That you've become Alexander Zaldostanov, martyr for Novorussia, fighting on behalf of the people's freedom. But I advise you to think carefully before you do, because it would only take me minutes to pull the plug, and things could get more complicated for you after that."

The tense silence of a baccarat room filled the shed where we found ourselves. A portrait of Stalin and a caricature of Obama gazed at us from the walls with shared indifference. Zaldostanov was thinking with a childish pout of concentration on his face. From time to time, he would run his hand distractedly over the cartridge belt he wore for decorative effect. It was hard to tell whether he was meditating on my words, or feeling for a bullet with my name on it, or just too drunk to do anything.

Then he rose slowly to his feet.

"Follow me, Vadya."

The biker went outside and led me silently toward some ruins by the vacant lot where the Night Wolves had their base. We walked past a row of orange garbage trucks that had been converted into war vehicles, with their back compartments cleared out and mortars installed. Up close, the ruins lost their generic aspect. You could make out the remains of household objects in the rubble: a dented refrigerator, a door handle, some colored fabrics. Zaldostanov climbed onto a small mound and scratched at the ground with his big Doc Martens as if he were looking for something.

"Ah, there's always at least one," he said, bending down to pick up a dirt-covered piece of pink plastic. "Check it out, Vadya. Why don't you take this back to your daughter?"

At first, I didn't recognize the object he was holding out to me. When I took it in my hand, I realized it was a doll. It was missing an arm, and I wondered whether it had been lost in the explosion or whether it had happened earlier. This small, broken, dirty object must have had a name once. And a little girl had spent whole afternoons playing with it.

———

I didn't manage to say a word during the entire military flight that brought me back to Moscow. Even once I was back in the Kremlin, I stayed silent. If a question was put to me, I answered, but no more. I didn't feel like arguing. My arguments were as pertinent as ever, yet this was where they'd brought me. I was the one with the ingenious solutions, yet I'd found myself explaining to a Cossack festooned with cartridge belts that he had to keep fighting the war, keep bombing hospitals and schools, even if he didn't feel like it, even if there was no reason to, because that's what the subtle plan that my subtle mind had devised required.

Better that I keep quiet. Better yet that I stop thinking. Stripped of my suppositions, the truth appeared for what it was. The tsar's empire was born of war, and it was logical that in the end it should turn back to war. It was the unshakable foundation of our power, its original vice. And if you thought about it, had we ever moved beyond it? Things could never have been any different. I'd known this from the start, and I'd chosen to accompany Putin down this road. I'd done it neither out of conviction nor out of personal interest. I'd done it out of curiosity. To test myself. Because, in the end, I had nothing better to do. It was still a better motivation than most of the others had, I'd told myself. Greed, frustration, the need for revenge, fanaticism, the desire to be dominant over one's fellow man. I might not change the world for the better, but I'd keep others from stepping in and making it worse. Things hadn't exactly worked out that way.

The war in Ukraine had been like everything else. I wasn't the one who'd wanted it. In fact, I'd voiced my strong opposition. But afterwards, after the tsar made his decision, I'd done everything in my power to see that the war succeeded. Out of habit. Out of pride. And because I could. That's how it had been from the start. With the bombs in Moscow and the war in Chechnya. With Khodorkovsky's arrest and the fall of Berezovsky. I'd wanted none of these things to happen. But they'd all benefited from my tireless efforts. I couldn't stand the idea of losing. And I'd been lucky, I'd almost always won. Now I finally held the trophy I deserved: a doll, smeared with dirt and rubble, whose name I would never know.

28

THE PERFECTLY SQUARE FACE of Sechin appeared in the opening of my office door.

"Might I disturb you for a moment, Vadim Alexeievich?"

If Igor had taken the trouble to come and see me, it could only be to deliver some very bad news. He took a circuitous route, asking about my trip to the Donbas, as if at least three intelligence services hadn't already given him the details. Then, fixing me with the eyes of a nocturnal raptor: "By the way, Vadim Alexeievich, you've heard about the Americans, haven't you?"

—What about the Americans?

—Apparently they've made a list of people who will no longer be allowed to set foot in the United States. Your name is on it.

Sechin watched me carefully, looking for the slightest sign of distress.

"I'm afraid you'll have to forget about New York
for the moment."

—Oh, the sanctions over Ukraine. So they've decided to go ahead with that?

—Starting Monday.

The chekist seemed satisfied. The fact that my
name was on the list had made his morning.

Obviously, it was a bit bothersome. It wasn't just
New York. There was also California, and Maine, and
Boulder, Colorado. Being banned from American soil
would deprive me of pleasures Sechin had no notion of.

"Oh, and I heard something else too."

At this point, Igor had a distracted expression that
I'd learned to recognize. It was the look he assumed
when he concentrated most intensely. He was about to
really inflict pain on me.

"Your name is also on the European list."

Asshole. That's why he'd taken the trouble to come
tell me in person: he wanted to see my face at the
exact moment I learned that I'd lost Europe. Basically,
I thought, this man knows nothing about me except
how to cause me pain.

A giant block of stone had started falling in me. A
piece of bedrock. It had just broken off from my chest
and was now hurtling through space. Inside. It was
falling in the darkness without ever touching bottom.
Europe. An inconceivable thing. Me, deprived of Europe, you understand?

I mobilized all the strength I had to deprive Sechin of even the slightest satisfaction. "Just as well, I was planning to start exploring new places anyway. But what about you, Igor, your castle in Umbria?"

That castle was the apple of his eye.

Sechin's face suddenly assumed a total lack of expression, a sign that he was feeling intense emotion.

"Bah, bunch of old stones, really. I'm actually building a replica of it, in the Caucasus."

The chekist turned on his heels. He'd accomplished his mission. For my part, I didn't have much choice. I picked up the phone and dictated a statement to the press secretary to be released the moment the sanctions were announced: "I consider it an Oscar, the crown of my political career. It indicates that I've served my country with honor."

Then I dialed the landline at home. Ksenia had no cell phone, obviously, but luckily she happened not to have gone out on that morning. I made arrangements to meet her at the airport.

A few hours later, we landed in my favorite city for our last European weekend. Driving toward the hotel, we observed the solemn procession of redbrick buildings that line the avenues of Stockholm. Here, the snow doesn't turn to black sludge as in Moscow, it stays inexplicably white, as if the Swedes had solved this problem too, along with so many others. People were walking on the sidewalks as you Europeans do, without haste or fear. Around four o'clock, when the tired winter sun finally gave up, the grandeur of the slightly haughty facades overlooking the frozen surface of the sea became more affable, suddenly softened by the charm of a thousand glowing windows being lit, one after another. Lighting from below, I thought, that's the real difference. In Russia, table lamps and floor lamps are practically nonexistent. When you walk around even the fanciest neighborhoods of Moscow or Saint Petersburg, what you'll see are the pitiless beams of ceiling lights shining from above. Ceiling fixtures are practical. You only have to flip a single switch for the entire room to be bathed in the same brutal and uniform light. And it works well with television, as there's no reflection on the screen and the tone harmonizes with the set's bluish glare.

Small, low lamps, on the other hand, are not handy. You have to switch them on one by one, and it takes at least three or four to generate as much light as a single ceiling fixture. But the play of shadows on the walls and furniture creates an atmosphere that's propitious for conversation and reading old books, for wood fires and chamber music. All of which are things that, even in your country, have been swept away by cell phone screens. But at least individual lamps preserve the illusion. You can look from the outside into these softly lit rooms, bathed in filtered light, and believe that the people who live there spend their time telling fairy tales—a luxury that Russians have never allowed themselves.

Trying to imagine what life would be like in one of these houses has always been a perversion of mine. In two days, the sanctions would take effect, and the fantasy would turn into an impossibility. Exile in reverse, the worst possible punishment for a person like me.

At that moment, I remembered Berezovsky, his last years in London. He'd never been able to rid himself of Russia. Nothing really mattered to him except the one true pleasure of Russian life: looking at reality head-on, unfiltered, in the raw light of a ceiling fixture. I'd have been able to let Russia go, in his place. If I were living in London. Or anywhere else in Europe, for that matter. I could have lived in one of those houses in the suburbs with a little wrought iron gate and two steps leading up to the front door. I'd have filled it with books, found the good coffee shop nearby, and a bar where I could drink whiskey in the evening. I'd have gone on the same walk almost every day, remembering Russia from time to time as a mother who devours her own children. She'd devoured my grandfather and my father, but she wouldn't devour me. I'd escaped her, been saved. Or not. It was too late for me in any case. But my daughter would be saved. Russia would not have gotten her.

That's not how things played out, and I had to face the facts. The time had come for me to renounce Europe's gentility, its dim lamplight that hides the world's cruelty. I'd always known, somewhere deep inside, that this moment would come. Ever since my eyes first met

the tsar's. There was nothing European in his gaze,
nothing soft. Just determination, a need that counte-
nanced no opposition.

The next morning, we woke up in a small suite at my
favorite hotel, a kind of country house perched on an
island in the middle of Stockholm. We had breakfast
on the pinewood deck, facing the opaque surface of the
sea. In the distance, the cargo cranes of the commercial
port gave us a glimpse of an active and turbulent world,
only a vague echo of which reached us, drowned in any
case by my sadness and Ksenia's indolence.

I looked at my life as though I were a free diver. I
could see it shining on the surface, but I was no longer
able to breathe. It had been twenty years since I had
breathed. Not that those years had flown past. No, I
had the impression of having lived a thousand lifetimes.
But I'd never breathed, not for a single moment. I'd
been holding my breath. Now I was starting to see my
destination far in the distance. That final point at which
there's no further need to choose, because all the choices
have been made and what's left is just a formality.

I'd planned to spend the day bemoaning my fate. I
thought I'd earned it. But I hadn't factored in Ksenia's
ferocious intelligence beside me. Even now that she
was disposed in my favor, it still represented a threat.
She would never let me lie to myself.

We were walking along the sea, on Djurgården Island. When we'd left the hotel an hour earlier, we'd strolled arm in arm, chatting away, but silence had since settled around us, and it now enveloped each of our gestures. Only our breath hung in the air, and the wind laden with the scent of deep, snow-filled forests.

I walked alone, lost in thought, and Ksenia followed a few steps behind. Ahead of us, nestled among birch trees, was an orange-colored house. With its small dormer windows and massive gray chimneys, it looked somewhat like the house of the good witch. Whoever does not live there, I said to myself, has clearly missed out on life.

Behind me, I suddenly heard the lapping of water. I turned around, half expecting to find a swan swimming against the waves. Instead, I saw Ksenia, completely submerged in the icy sea, smiling at me with a challenge in her eyes. Her hastily removed clothing made multicolored splotches on the snow.

We looked at each other for a long moment—me, completely dressed on the shore, her, completely naked in the water. Her eyes were as deep as questions with no answer, but her mouth sketched a smile. I started to undress in turn. The gray fur-lined hat. The black English-made shoes that accompanied me everywhere. The suit and dark turtleneck. Ksenia watched me from the sea, but just before I dove in she turned and started swimming toward the open water. Once again, I was gripped with fear. Where was she going? I tried to call her. Had she forgotten that she was pregnant?

She had no intention of listening to me. My only option was to follow. I dove in noisily. It was the opposite of Ksenia's imperceptible splash. I may have screamed—bathing in icy water has never been my forte. I instinctively started swimming, as much to keep from freezing in place as to catch up with Ksenia. She had stopped about fifty yards from shore and was waiting for me. On the point of reaching her, I thought she was going to take off again. But no, she waited for me to come up. And there, while I pressed her luminous body against mine in the dark water, I read for the first time in her eyes the full majesty of the mystery growing inside her. A fierce and unlimited freedom had been her one goal, for which she had formerly been willing to submit to the most abject slavery. But at present nothing could deviate her from the course the stars had traced for her, and though she was crueler even than before, a new tenderness had ripened in her breast, which I felt was destined for no one but me. All other sensations fell away from me at this point, like ripe fruit dropping from a tree, and alone at the deepest core of my being there remained a reverence for the splendor of the unknown life that vibrated in front of me. And for the first time in years, while the ice pushed against us from every side and the current threatened to carry us away, I had the feeling of being able once more to breathe.

29

FAMILIARITY CAN LEAD TO errors in judgment.
For years, in the Kremlin, Stalin and the rest of the
nomenklatura lived elbow to elbow. They all had large
apartments that had once belonged to the tsar's high
officials, and they always dined together. Stalin would
seek them out to play chess or organize a small dinner
among friends. He never took the seat of honor but
sat at the end of the table, and if something had to be
fetched from the kitchen, he would be the one to rise
and get it. There was also a small movie theater. The
children rode on their bicycles and kicked a ball around.
They'd grown up together, as if they were a family.
Which didn't stop Stalin from eliminating them one
after another. In fact, it made his task easier. Nobody
could believe that Koba, as they called him, would
have them arrested, tortured, and killed. Proximity led
them astray. They formed the illusion that a friendship

of twenty years would stop the leader from doing what he had to do. But that's not how it works. The leader follows his intuition, he has a predator's instinct for survival. And in the final analysis, the only thing that can guarantee his survival is the death of everyone else around him.

In my case, I left first. I didn't let myself be fooled by familiarity. A prince's confidence is not a privilege but a death sentence: when a man confides his secret to another, he becomes his slave, and rulers don't consent to slavery. The urge to break the mirror that reflects our image back to us is a common enough feeling. Also, a prince can return small favors, but when they become too large and he no longer knows how to repay them, he may be tempted to solve the problem by eliminating its cause.

The tsar had no affection for others, at best he grew used to them. And at a certain point, he lost the habit of seeing me. At his dacha in Novo-Ogaryovo, he had the forest cleared for three kilometers in every direction. He would rise late in the morning, breakfast on fresh eggs that Patriarch Kirill sent him, then exercise in his gym watching the news on a screen. If there was anything urgent, it was there that he would read the confidential briefing materials and issue his instructions. After that he would swim a kilometer in the pool. The first visitors of the day—ministers, advisors, or corporate CEOs, who'd been summoned the night before—would wait patiently on the pool deck for the tsar to emerge from the water so they could hand him his robe and briefly discuss some matter or other.

Only in the early afternoon would the presidential motorcade head for the Kremlin. The streets were closed to traffic a half hour ahead of time, and a police car at every crossing ensured that the tsar's solitude would not be breached. Traveling from Novo-Ogaryovo to the Kremlin, Putin crossed almost the entire capital, which froze to a halt while he passed through. The real workday began when he arrived in the office, and it often lasted until the first streaks of dawn. The tsar's whole life was out of phase with the lives of normal people, and it had a distorting effect on everyone who worked with him. One man didn't sleep at night, and he'd trained all those who counted for anything in Moscow to share his vigil until three or four in the morning. Knowing the leader's nocturnal habits, a hundred or so ministers, high officials, and generals stuck around, waiting for his call. And each kept a small squadron of assistants and secretaries on hand. So the lights in the ministries stayed lit, and Moscow's powerful once again lost their sleep, as they had in Stalin's time.

The one true obligation at court is to be present. Being there, always, each time there's even a faint possibility that the sovereign's gaze might fall upon you. For my part, I never went to Novo-Ogaryovo with a light heart. The disagreeably sporty atmosphere saddened me. Every time I had the chance, I would arrange for someone else to go in my stead, and God knows there was no lack of candidates! After my return from Stockholm, I hardly ever set foot there again. And I got into the habit of going to bed at night when I was tired without bothering to leave my phone on. The tsar once or twice had me dragged out of bed by the head of the presidential guard. But it was clear that things couldn't go on this way. The tsar found it intolerable that proximity to him was no longer the source of all my joys.

One day, at the Kremlin, during a meeting where I found myself as usual in the minority, the tsar pierced me with a look of perfect indifference, as though I didn't exist.

"You think you're the cleverest of us all, Vadya. But do you know what the truth is? If you stay young for too long, you end up aging badly."

He was right. Forty is an unforgiving age. Everything is revealed, and you can't hide anymore. The truth is that even when I came closest to the summit of power, I'd never stopped being a marginal figure. Basically, I think it comes down to Grandfather's library again. It made me aware that I was not at the center of time. Our epoch, exciting as it may be, is only the umpteenth version of the comedy whose many variations have unfolded over the course of the centuries. "From time to time, a man rises up in the world, displays his fortune, and proclaims: It is I! His glory lives for the duration of an interrupted dream, and already death arises and proclaims: It is I!"

Without ever having set foot there, and three centuries ago, La Bruyère described the Kremlin of today more accurately than our best journalists have, or yours. If I hadn't been aware of him, I would never have been able to accomplish the work I did. I'd have stayed on the surface. My contribution to the tsar's cause would have been less effective, less decisive, if I can say that. But it was also what eventually brought about my self-condemnation. Suddenly, I saw my life as it actually was: an endless struggle with the angel of negligence, of unjustified brutality, and of ungovernable appetite. Twenty years in service to it. It could have been twenty days, it could have been twenty minutes. Same thing.

If I'd been one of the gang, then why not. But I'd always been an outsider. When I was a boy, my grandfather would sometimes tell me about those wolves that leave the pack for no apparent reason. They go their own way, alone. Some end up forming a new pack. Others not. They roam the forest or cross the steppes, always alone. And they don't seem to suffer from their isolation. They live their lives apart, and over time they develop their own habits, which are different from those of the pack. Hunters have learned to be wary of them. They know that solitary wolves are stronger, smarter, and more aggressive than the others.

Clearly Grandfather thought of himself as one of them. Who knows, maybe it's a recessive trait, fated to reappear every other generation. One thing for certain is that it's not a trait the pack approves of—they can accept anything except independence. Afterwards, all sorts of things were said about me. That I had a swelled head. That I'd been caught with my hand in the till. Even that I'd wanted to take the tsar's place. For some, calumny is the only form of imagination.

The truth is that I've always conspired on behalf of power, never against it. That's my nature, something many people don't understand. It's true that among those who surround the powerful there are always some who want to take their place. But a genuine advisor is of a different order than a man in power. The fact is, the advisor is lazy. His words, when they are whispered in the ruler's ear, achieve a maximum effect without his ever having to weary himself with rising through the ranks. Having said his piece, he goes happily back to his library, while the ferocious beasts continue to rip each other apart under the water's surface. He has a splinter of ice in his heart: as the others grow more heated, he becomes cooler. It can sometimes end badly, because what disturbs the powerful most is autonomy. But when I tendered my resignation, the tsar had other things on his mind. I think he viewed it with relief: he no longer needed me. Inventing a new order of government requires a certain level of imagination, but seeing it implemented takes only a servant's blind devotion.

No one replaced me. The Labrador retriever was the only advisor Putin completely trusted. He took her running on the grounds of his dacha and brought her along to the office. Otherwise, the tsar was completely alone. From time to time, a guard would appear, or a servant, or a courtier who'd been called in for one reason or another. That was it. There was no woman at his side, no children. As to friends, he knew that at the stage he'd reached, the very idea of having friends was unimaginable. The tsar lived in a world where even the best of friends turned into courtiers or implacable enemies, and most often both at once.

In the West, your leaders are like teenagers, they can't bear to be alone, they're always wanting someone to see them. You get the impression that if they had to spend a whole day in a room, deprived of company, they'd dissolve into the atmosphere like a gust of warm air. Our tsar, on the other hand, lives in solitude and thrives on it. Contemplation is what gives him the strength that surprises so many of your observers. With time, he's become an element, almost, like the sky or the wind. You've forgotten what it means to live as an adult, anchored in reality. You think a leader is a kind of master of ceremonies, you want leaders who are like you, who are on your level. Distance preserves authority. Like God, the tsar can elicit enthusiasm in others, but he can never feel enthusiasm himself; his nature is necessarily indifferent. His face has already acquired the marble-like pallor of immortality.

At this level, we have moved well beyond the desire for a fancy funeral that I spoke of earlier. The tsar's ideal would be more like a cemetery in which he stood alone, vertical, the sole survivor among all his enemies and even all his friends, relatives, and children. Even Koni, maybe. And all other living creatures. "Caligula wished that all men had but one neck, that he might reduce the whole world to nothing with a single blow." Power in its pure state. That's what the tsar has become. Or maybe he was that way from the start. The only throne that will bring him peace is death.

30

RUSSIA IS THE WEST'S nightmare machine. At the end of the nineteenth century, your intellectuals dreamed of revolution. We had one. You never did more than talk about Communism. We experienced it for seventy years. Then came the era of capitalism. And even there, we went a lot further than you. In the 1990s no one deregulated, privatized, or gave more scope to entrepreneurial initiative than we. Here the biggest fortunes were built, starting from nothing, without rules or limits. We really believed in it, but it didn't work.

Now, it's starting all over again. Your system is in danger because you're no longer able to exercise power. Believe me, as someone who has experienced power firsthand, I don't have much fondness for it. Grandfather used to say that somebody should collect all the equestrian statues in all the towns of the world and

send them to the middle of the desert, to a site dedi-
cated to all the perpetrators of massacres throughout
history. I've always felt he was right, and I can tell you
that the years I spent in the Kremlin didn't make me
change my mind. Just the opposite.

Today, however, power is the only solution, because its goal, the goal of all active power, is to abolish
events. "A housefly, should it fly inopportunely during
a ceremony, humiliates the tsar," said Custine. Even the
smallest event that occurs outside the control of power
can spell its death, or the possibility of its death.

Human nature is greedy for events. It watches for
them, covets them, even if it seems to be afraid of
them, but it's clear this is a taste we can no longer in-
dulge. Because today an event, even the tiniest hop of
a fly, can set off Armageddon. The virus was a dress
rehearsal for this, but it was only the beginning. From
now on, a race will be underway between events and
power. And since the former will always raise the possibility of the apocalypse, we will be obliged to choose
the latter. Not the sort of pseudopower that you have
in the West: clown masks acting out a tragic script. No,
power returning to its primal origins: the pure exercise
of force. The marble statue protecting with one hand
and threatening with the other.

Up till now, power has always been imperfect. Because it has had to rely on human agency to realize its
promise. And man is weak, always.

In every revolution there's a decisive moment: that instant when the troops rebel against the government and refuse to shoot. It's Putin's nightmare, as it was the nightmare of all the tsars before him. The risk that the troops, instead of firing on the crowd, will join forces with them is the ever-present threat looming over every power. That's why when the students started to occupy Tiananmen Square, Deng Xiaoping wisely chose not to respond right away. He knew that he was at the precipice's edge. He didn't want to risk exposing his troops to the protesters with their slogans, their chants, their pretty girls making eyes at the soldiers. He preferred to wait, to bring in soldiers from across the country who didn't speak Mandarin, so that they couldn't join forces with the protesters. It took those troops several days to arrive, but when they did they were implacable.

Now let's imagine a power that doesn't need to rely on human collaboration anymore. Its security—and its military force—are guaranteed by instruments that are incapable of rebelling against it. An army of sensors, of drones, of robots capable of striking at any moment, without the slightest hesitation. That, finally, would be power in its absolute form. As long as it is founded on the collaboration of flesh-and-blood men, every power, no matter how steel-fisted, is dependent on their consent. But once it relies on machines to maintain order and enforce discipline, it will be free of all restraint.

The problem with machines is not that they'll rebel against their human masters but that they'll follow their orders to the letter.

It's important always to look at where things come from. All the technologies that have suddenly appeared in our lives in the past few years have their origin in the military. Computers were developed during World War II to decode enemy ciphers. The internet was conceived as a means of communication in the event of a nuclear war, GPS started as a way of locating combat units, and so on. They are all technologies intended for command and control, not freedom. Only a bunch of Californians high on LSD could be idiotic enough to think that a tool invented by the military could be transformed into an instrument of liberation. Yet many of them believed exactly that.

But at this point it's clear, right? You see it too. The truth is that the military technology surrounding us has created the conditions for universal mobilization. Now, wherever we are, we can be identified, called to order, neutralized if necessary. The solitary individual, free will, and even democracy have all become obsolete. The increase in data has made all of humanity one nervous system, a mechanism made of standard, predictable configurations, like a vast flock of birds or a school of fish.

We are not yet at war, but we are already militarized. This was a dream of the Soviets. Our state has always been based on mobilization. We were a nation entirely founded on the idea of war, on the defense of the homeland against possible attacks from abroad. All the sacrifices, all the many infringements on freedom, were justified on that basis: the defense of a greater freedom, that of the motherland. In the 1950s, the KGB devised a plan to put on file all the contacts of every Soviet citizen. My father's *vertushka* was the symbol of it. But Facebook went much further. The Silicon Valley crew went far beyond the dreams of the old Soviet bureaucrats. There's no limit to the surveillance they managed to put in place. Thanks to them, every moment in our lives has become a source of information.

The Nazis used to say that the only person in Germany who was still a private individual was a sleeping one, but Silicon Valley has outdone them too. The physiological changes that people undergo, even in their sleep, are no longer secret. They've all been converted into data. Till now it's only been used to generate profit, but tomorrow it may be used to exercise the most implacable control that man has ever known.

The mobilization has up to this point been benevolent. It relied on our laziness and supplied us with shiny glass beads, in exchange for which we've sold our freedom. But when the next virus erupts from a market or a laboratory, when Seattle, Hamburg, or Yokohama are destroyed by a dirty bomb or a biological weapon, when a random kid who is disaffected with life can, instead of opening fire on his classmates, destroy a city, all of humanity will ask for one thing only: protection.

Security, at all costs. Already today, variations from the norm are suspect, and soon the tiniest deviation will signal an enemy, a person slated for elimination. And the infrastructure will already be in place. The mobilization, which has been commercial up till now, will become political and military. All of the instruments at our disposal will need to be harnessed in the fight against the apocalypse. Faced with terror, everything else will be bearable.

On that day, the world will be ready for the coming of Zamyatin's Benefactor—the one who will ensure that nothing further happens. Machines will have enabled power to exist in its absolute form. A single man will then be able to dominate all of humanity. And it will be an ordinary person, without particular talent, because power will no longer reside in man but in machines, and a randomly picked man will be able to make them function.

His reign will not last long—a dictator being, as our Brodsky used to say, just an old-fashioned version of a computer. In a world governed by robots, it's only a matter of time before the figure at the apex is replaced by a robot.

For a long time we believed that machines were man's instrument, but it's now clear that men were the instruments that paved the way for machines. The transition will happen slowly: machines won't subject men to their rule, but they'll enter man, like an urge, an intimate aspiration. Even now, becoming a flawless machine is the governing ideal of billions of men, who struggle to meld ever more completely into technology's flux.

Human history ends with us. With you, with me, and maybe with our children. Afterwards, there will still be something, but it won't be humanity. The beings that come after us, if there are any, will have different ideas and preoccupations than those that have engaged man until now.

We will have been the parenthesis that has allowed the descent of God into the world. Except that God, instead of taking the improbable form of a disembodied being, will be a gigantic artificial organism, created by man but capable after a while of transcending him to fulfill the prophecy of a time without sin and without pain.

Behold, the tabernacle of God is with men,
And he will dwell with them, and they shall be his people,
And God himself shall be with them, and be their God.
And God shall wipe away all tears from their eyes;
And there shall be no more death,
Neither sorrow, nor crying,
Neither shall there be any more pain:
For the former things are passed away.

And what if the prophets' visions were to come true? What if man's torments were but a necessary prologue to God's arrival? What are a few thousand years of suffering, on the scale of the history of the universe—or even of Planet Earth? No, it isn't God who creates, but God who is created. Each day, like humble workers in the vineyards of the Lord, we create the conditions for his coming. Already, we have conferred on the machine the greater part of the attributes that the ancients assigned to the Lord. There was a time when God saw everything and recorded everything in anticipation of the Last Judgment; he was the supreme archivist. The machine has now taken his place. Its memory is infinite, its capacity for decision-making infallible. All that's missing is immortality and the resurrection, but we're getting there. The image of a warrior God battling the final enemy, death, as it appears in the apocalypse of the prophet Isaiah, is in reality—we can now confirm this—an image of the computer engaged in devising the final algorithm.

One final transition remains. The recognition that technology has become metaphysics. I don't know how long it will take, but the path has been traced out. So you see, I lied to you at the beginning, the real race is not between power and the apocalypse, but between the coming of the Lord and the apocalypse.

31

THE ROOM WAS PLUNGED into silence. The fire in the big stone fireplace, which Baranov had till then been feeding with an occasional log, had stopped crackling, robbing the library of the glow that had so struck me on my arrival. Casting a look around, I felt myself to be the last survivor of a very ancient catastrophe. Baranov's books, his elegant walnut desk, the lecterns, the globes, all belonged to a past era. Having finished his tale, Baranov himself had taken on the consistency of one of those ash-covered bodies you find in the ruins of Pompeii. Seated across from me, he gave the impression of having never needed to breathe.

At that moment, there was a creaking at the far end of the room, and a small chestnut-haired head poked through the door.

—I can't sleep, Daddy.

—Then stay here with us.

A child of four or five, still a bit sleepy-eyed and dressed in a light flannel nightshirt, entered the room. She looked like a small brioche, barely out of the oven. The sharp, delicate features of her face contrasted with the still-dreaming expression of her almond eyes, now starting to percolate with curiosity at finding a stranger in the study at this hour. After throwing her arms around her father's neck, she went and sat on the rug, near a hassock on which a large striped cat was sleeping.

I'd turned my eyes away for a moment, and when I looked at Baranov again, his face was completely transformed. He was no longer the same person.

—All the happiness I've known in the world is concentrated here, in a three-foot-six-inch frame.

In front of us, the little girl spoke quietly to the cat. From what I could tell, she seemed to be translating bits and pieces of our conversation for its benefit, afterwards going on to other, more private topics that concerned only the two of them. She raised her eyes from time to time to her father with the boundless confidence of protected children, who are still ignorant of the evil they will sooner or later encounter. Baranov, in turn, looked in her direction as though no point on earth had ever possessed such luminous intensity.

—We're considering buying a dog. It's not really something I've ever had much interest in. But for how much longer will I still be able to make her happy?

I then understood. No other thought now occupied the mind of this man who had been the most powerful strategist in the Kremlin. The bright eyes of a child of five ruled over his skeptical nature more completely than even the tsar had ever managed to.

—Before Anja, I don't think I ever experienced fear. Now I live in terror, starting from the moment I first saw her. She put her fingers to my lips and I understood then that my life was in her hands and not the opposite. The Russian spoke this in a murmur, as if he'd once again read my thoughts.

The child smiled at him from the carpet where she sat cross-legged. She was waiting for her life to start. And in the meantime, she wasn't sorry to spend time with this calm, massive man who clearly wanted nothing more than the chance to accompany her a little further.

—I have very little to teach her. She's really the one who teaches me to look the moment in the face. My daughter doesn't count the hours, or the days. She's given me the gift of the present, which I was unfamiliar with, having always lived in the future. Someday, though, we'll have to part. My only duty is to lead her to the threshold, then to let her enter alone, withdrawing with a slight nod. She's still only a child, yet I can't keep from thinking every day about that goodbye. I only hope that I'll have the strength for it. That I'll manage to smile. That I won't ruin everything with an awkward expression. I'd like her to remember me as a smiling presence.

His daughter was the one exception to Baranov's immoderate need for solitude. Each moment that he lived in her company represented a small miracle that the Russian had never imagined he would deserve. Nothing in his life as a lazy arriviste justified it. And yet the child was there, working on a complicated abstract drawing, with that look of concentration and pride he liked more than anything. Watching her, Baranov already felt nostalgia for her. In those moments, gratitude flooded through him like a hit of vodka and kept him from harming himself. He would have liked to precede her into the world, if only for a moment, to whisper to the wind the news of her coming and blanket the streets ahead of her with flowers.

—Before this child arrived, no one was ever able to really count on me. Neither my family, nor my friends, nor the tsar, nor even Ksenia. People and events passed through me leaving no trace, a corridor in the middle of a house. All my life, I only wanted to test myself on the vastest possible field of action. Now the moment in my life has arrived to make smaller circles. Not to pretend to cover the whole world, but to choose a fragment of it instead. And to make it live, instead of looking to master it. There's nothing more conservative than a child, you know, the rapture of repetition, which is the first of all passions. I have to stay completely still, so as not to harm her.

Across from us, Anja had set aside her drawing and returned to playing with the cat, who gamely but

without much enthusiasm pretended to be interested in
a small cloth rabbit that the child was wiggling under
its nose.

—Daddy, what do you think Pasha would say if he
could talk?

—"I'd have more fun with a real rabbit."

—Daddy!

—No, I was joking. He would say, "I like being
with you, Anja, I love you more than anything."

I got to my feet in silence, nodding briefly toward
the man who'd shared the tsar's insomniac nights for
fifteen years. Baranov shot me a grateful look. From
the moment his daughter had entered the room, our
conversation had stopped interesting him. I crossed
the darkened drawing rooms, where only the ticking
of the grandfather clock could be heard. The light of
dawn cast a faint glow on the portraits hanging on the
walls, the furniture from Karelia, and the white porce-
lain woodstoves. Once in the entry hall, I crossed the
threshold and the heavy oak door of the Baranov house
shut behind me. Outside, snow was falling gently.

Acknowledgments

Thanks to Thea, my first reader, without whom many things would not exist, including this book.

GIULIANO DA EMPOLI is an Italian and Swiss writer and journalist. He was Deputy Mayor for Culture in Florence and a senior advisor to Italian prime minister Matteo Renzi. Since the publication of his first book at the age of twenty-two, he has published eleven more books on the economy and its social and political consequences. *The Wizard of the Kremlin* won the Grand Prix du Roman and was a finalist for the Goncourt Prize.

WILLARD WOOD grew up in France and has translated more than thirty works of fiction and nonfiction from the French. He has won the Lewis Galantière Award for Literary Translation and received a National Endowment for the Arts Fellowship in Translation. His recent translations include Camille de Toledo's *Theseus, His New Life* (Other Press, 2023) and Patrick Boucheron's *Trace and Aura* (Other Press, 2022).